Surviving Haley

Brenda Baker

Brenda Baker

Surviving Haley

Contact Information: titleadmin@pelicanbookgroup.com

Cover Art by *Nicola Martinez*

Watershed Books, a division of Pelican Ventures, LLC
www.pelicanbookgroup.com PO Box 1738 *Aztec, NM * 87410

Watershed Books praise and splash logo is a trademark of Pelican Ventures, LLC

Publishing History
First Watershed Edition, 2015
Paperback Edition ISBN 978-1-61116-482-4
Electronic Edition ISBN 978-1-61116-481-7
Published in the United States of America

Dedication

In memory of Beatrice Andrews and Gretchen Baker
who were always there for me.

This novel would never have been completed without
the encouragement, dedication, and insights offered
by: Helene Prevost, Diane Owens, Donna Koppelman,
Janet Skoog, Dorothy Ray, Becky Berg, Paula Jolin and
Barbara Ostguard. I appreciate all of you!

Thank you to my agent, Steven Hutson for believing in
my work, and to Ruth Hutson for her assistance.
Special thanks to Nicola Martinez, Editor-in-Chief at
Pelican Book Group, for wanting to publish the story,
and to Jamie West, my editor, who was just an email
away, and whose suggestions improved the book.

To my family and friends, thank you for standing by
me. And thank you, God for making this all possible.

1

The first night in our new house, my mother watched every sporkful of food I lifted to my mouth. This was her new mission: controlling my diet. Make that: controlling my life. I had gained some weight since the accident. OK, I was fat. Blimp status fat. But my mother had appointed herself the food warden, and I hadn't even advertised the position.

We sat on boxes labeled "kitchen," printed with black marker in my mother's neat handwriting. We'd scooted them next to our rickety card table because our furniture hadn't arrived yet, even though the moving company promised it'd be here by now. The kitchen was smaller than our old one. The whole house was smaller. But so was our family.

I reached tentatively for another piece of chicken, waiting for my mother to say something. Right when my fingers closed around a drumstick—baked not fried—she said, "Lauren, don't you think you've had enough?"

Yes, if I had a stomach the size of a gerbil's.

I dropped the chicken and snatched a carrot stick instead. Vegetables were acceptable. I could eat all the veggies I wanted, as long as I didn't dip them in anything that tasted good, like ranch dressing.

Dad cleared his throat and shook his head, barely enough to notice, but Mom caught it.

She crumpled her napkin and flung it on her

Styrofoam plate, then pushed her "fragile, handle with care" seat away from the table, folded the flaps in on the Crispy Chicken box, and shoved it out of sight in the refrigerator abandoned by the previous owners.

I'd bet a hundred dollars Mom had counted the remaining pieces of chicken, so a middle-of-the-night raid was out.

"Well," Dad said, smiling and looking straight at me. "I'll do the dishes." He dumped the chicken bones, napkins, and sporks onto one plate, stacked the other two beneath it, and stuffed the whole mess into the brown paper chicken sack. "I think I saw the Wii someplace. How about it, Lauren? You up for a game?"

Mom sighed and stopped wiping the card table in circular strokes with a dampened paper towel. "Tell your father we have to finish unloading the truck. Then you need to take a shower and get to bed. You don't want to be late for your first day of school."

This was how she talked to him now, "tell your father," like I was the interpreter. It had been like this ever since Dad decided we were moving. He said it would be the best thing for all of us. We needed to start over in a new place, so we could move forward with our lives.

Dad opened his mouth to speak, but I cut him off. "It's fine. We can play tomorrow. I'll start hauling in stuff."

Before we left Minnesota, we'd crammed everything we could into the back of Dad's pick-up truck.

"Be out in a second to help you," Dad said.

I pushed through the back door and meandered to the truck. Yanking the tailgate open, I stared at the ten-plus plastic bags and the tape-sealed boxes. The wind caught my hair and it whipped around my face. Mom had tagged the twist-tied sacks, and I shoved two marked "bedding" toward the tailgate. The sacks were extra-capacity size and incredibly heavy.

"Toss them down to me," Dad said. "We'd better hurry, looks like a storm's coming." Black clouds hovered overhead. The temperature had dropped since we'd arrived, and a cool breeze carried the scent of rain. Dad bent over and grabbed the sacks. For the zillionth time, I saw the rose tattoo on his upper arm with three names on it: "Lydia, Lauren, Haley," but I turned away, because seeing Haley's name hurt too much.

He carried those sacks inside and Mom plodded over to take the next ones. My parents hauled, and I kept shoving our belongings to the end of the truck bed.

The maple tree in the front yard bowed in the wind. Raindrops plopped on my forehead as I picked up a box and carried it to the tailgate. A flash of lightning slashed a jagged white line through the darkened sky. Ten minutes later, rain pelted us, but we kept working until only three boxes remained. We each carried one, me leading the way. When I'd almost reached the door, I slipped on the slick concrete and my box hit the porch. That was when I noticed the label: "Haley's things."

"Be careful with that!" My mother handed off her box to Dad. She dropped to her hands and knees and slid Haley's box close to herself. It was pouring now, the rain drenching our hair and clothes, but Mom slumped against the house, cradling the box and blocking the doorway so we couldn't get past her.

Dad set down his load and lay a hand on her back.

She pushed him away without even looking at him.

"Lydia," he said, "let's go inside."

Without a word, she rose and gathered the box in her arms. Dad opened the door for her and she shuffled through it.

Dad and I crossed the threshold, our sandals wet, our cargo soggy and damp smelling. Puddles collected around our feet on the tiled entryway.

Upstairs, a door closed, and I knew we wouldn't see Mom for the rest of the night.

"She hates me," I said. "When is she going to stop hating me?"

He smiled, but it was a sad smile. The skin around his eyes crinkled. "She doesn't hate you. Don't ever think that. Just give her some time, OK?"

How much time? It had already been a month since the accident. I chewed my thumbnail down to a stub. I needed chocolate and I needed it now. Something gooey. Knowing my mother, she'd pitched everything remotely sweet, but she didn't know about the crunch bars I'd bought at the Gas 'N' Go and hidden in my purse.

Dad wrapped his arm around me and tightened his fingers against my shoulder. "We love you, honey. Remember that. Now, find a towel and go take your shower. I'll call you for school in the morning."

"OK."

He loved me, yeah. But Mom, well, I'd changed her life forever. For Mom, there was no magic left...no more Santa Claus or Tooth Fairy or Easter Bunny. Without Haley, she couldn't buy toys or play at the park or watch cartoons or animated movies, because she had no reason to anymore.

I ripped open a garbage bag, thankful our bedding and towels were dry, and headed upstairs. A narrow line of light glowed under the master bedroom door. No sound came from the room. Was Mom sitting in there on the floor, hugging Haley's box?

After showering, I trudged to my room across the hallway, closed my door, and spread a blanket on the floor before I dumped out the contents of my purse. A cellphone, a coin purse, sticky notes where I'd scribbled down reminders to myself, a billfold with a meager amount of cash, and of course what I was really searching for: a crunch bar.

In less than thirty seconds, I'd devoured a whole bar, swallowing the creamy rich chocolate, the taste lingering on my tongue. I had four more, but I couldn't afford to eat them all tonight. They were my insurance for the next week or so until I had a chance to buy more. For several minutes, I felt better. Good, almost. But it didn't last. It never lasted.

Gathering my stuff into a pile, I shoved it back inside my purse and collapsed against the blanket. The new carpet smell made my eyes water. This was usually a good smell, but not when it was right next to my nose. The floor pressed into my back, and my stomach bulged above the waistband of my pajamas.

Were Mom and Dad in the same room? Doubtful. As far as I knew, they hadn't slept together since the accident.

Outside, rain spit against the windows. Thunder rattled the glass panes. The streetlight blinked off along with every light in our house. Darkness swallowed my room. *Welcome to Nebraska.*

2

My new school sprawled across a straw-yellow lawn. According to the weather guy on Channel Seven, the late-summer heat spell would end soon, and people didn't need to water their grass, because it was dormant, not dead. An American flag capped a Goliath-sized pole; red, white, and blue fluttered in the wind. Inside, students streamed past the glassed-in hallway visible from the street.

Even though it was only 7:30 a.m. and about sixty-five degrees outside, sweat ran down my back. My hair clung to my neck.

Dad killed the engine and pressed the volume control on the radio until the song faded away. Leaning back against the headrest, he closed his eyes and sighed. "I know this is hard. You want me to wait?"

"For what?" Did he think he needed to take my hand and walk me to the door? I was starting ninth grade not kindergarten. Still, it was sweet of him to offer.

"Well, OK, then," he said smiling, "I guess you're fine."

Fine. Right. I could do this. I grabbed my book bag, rested my fingers on the door handle, and cracked the truck door open. So what if I didn't know anybody? That was the whole point in moving…nobody knew me either.

"Good luck, kiddo. Have a great day."

Dad has always called me "kiddo." But he'd called Haley "Princess," because she was—Mom and Dad's little princess. Whenever I closed my eyes, I pictured her long blonde hair with a touch of curl at the ends, and her huge green eyes fringed with dark lashes like she'd used lots of mascara, but of course, five-year-olds didn't use make-up. *Stop it. Don't think about Haley. Not today.*

Lines creased Dad's face, more lines than a thirty-five-year-old guy should have. He looked so…old. The dark circles under his eyes. The streaks of gray in his hair.

Last night, I'd woken to the sound of floorboards creaking in the hallway. Someone had switched on the hall light—probably Dad. He couldn't sleep again. Insomnia must be contagious, because after I woke up, it took me another hour to fall back asleep.

"Bye, Dad." I heaved myself out of the passenger seat and turned to slam the door shut.

He leaned forward and peered out at me. "Lauren?"

I bit my lip. *Please don't say it. Don't say it wasn't my fault, because it was.* "Yeah?"

"You look beautiful. I love you," he said.

Truth: Dads, if they love you, will lie about your appearance. I knew this was the case, because two new zits studded my forehead, my hair was a tangled mess, and my clothes had more wrinkles than an octogenarian. "I love you, too."

When the truck pulled away from the curb, it traveled several blocks before it turned left and disappeared from sight. I was on my own. New school. New life. I didn't deserve either.

As I ambled to the front double doors, I felt my stomach hanging over the waistband of my jeans like an over-inflated inner tube. I swallowed, forced a couple of deep breaths, and headed for the building, my pulse racing. I'd almost reached the door when the button on my jeans popped off and rolled several feet across the sidewalk. It came to rest beside a guy who leaned against the building, talking with a friend. The guy wore a gray tee-shirt with a small cross logo and the letters "WWJD." I'd been around enough church kids to know what it meant: "What would Jesus do?" Answer: Absolutely nothing. He didn't save Haley.

"Dude, you lose something?" the guy's friend said. He stooped and plucked the button from the sidewalk.

"Don't think so," the guy said. He pivoted and faced me.

For one second our eyes locked, and I thought I might melt like the Wicked Witch of the West, even though nobody had doused me with water. Water was exactly what I needed though, because my face felt like it had a first-degree burn. His eyes—think cerulean blue—made my breath catch in my throat, and then he smiled at me, and my knees turned to gelatin. His light brown hair was streaked with blond strands bleached by the sun, and it brushed the tops of his shoulders.

Do not look at the runaway button. Think chameleon, blend in. Not easy when my zipper was inching downward, and I didn't have a clue where I was going. Ducking my head, I scuttled past the guys and went inside.

Kids clustered in the hallway. Random conversations bounced off the walls. Everybody had somebody to talk to except me. My feet felt like hundred-pound weights. I pulled the schedule they'd mailed me from my backpack and scanned it. First period, History, Room 110. Luckily, the room was easy to find. Most of the seats were empty when I got there. I skulked to the back row, keeping my head bowed because my face was still warm from the lost button fiasco. Zipper teeth bit into my stomach.

After squeezing into a chair, the kind with an attached desk, a scary scenario flashed through my mind: What if my hips wedged tight between the chair and the desk? What if the teacher had to call the janitor to come and pry me out?

A girl sauntered in wearing tight-butt, low-rise jeans, a stretchy tee shirt and a deep purple pedicure with tiny white flowers on her big toes. Every boy in the room gawked and practically drooled as the girl model-walked her way to the front of the class.

"Hey, Tiffany," a tall, preppy-looking girl said. "Sit here." She pointed to an unoccupied desk next to her.

An easy smile played across Tiffany's lip-glossed mouth. She sank gracefully into the seat and sat reed-straight in the chair, her head held high, and one long jean-clad leg bobbed up and down.

"OK, people, listen up." The teacher rapped a pointer stick against the whiteboard. Then he crossed his arms, still holding the stick as if it were a weapon, and slid onto a corner of his desk, causing a book to thud against the floor. When he looked momentarily frazzled and stooped to retrieve the book, I smiled, until Tiffany shot me a glare that would have withered a plant. In every school, there were kids who thought they belonged to a superior species. This concept was completely alien to me, but whatever. No amount of deodorant could have stopped the sweat that broke out under my pits.

"This is Room 110," the teacher bellowed, slamming the book back onto his desk. "American History. If you do not see Room 110 on your schedule, leave. Now!" The guy had a thick neck, deep-set, dark eyes, and he stared at us like a buffalo ready to charge because we'd invaded his space. The overhead lights reflected in the bald spot on the top of his head.

Tiffany glanced at the friend who'd saved her the seat, both of them struggling to hide their laughter.

I didn't smile this time. With one look, Tiffany had put me in my place, as in, I was not in her league and never would be.

"Nobody?" the teacher said. "Very good. You can all read. That's a start. My name is Mr. Hazzard. I will call out your assigned seats. When you hear your name, please move."

Great, assigned seats. This usually meant sitting next to people you couldn't stand for an entire school year. Plus the hypothesis was about to be tested: Could I slide out of my seat without getting stuck?

Mr. Hazzard droned through the alphabet and when he got to the V's, and said, "Vancleave," Tiffany stood and did a runway walk to the back row.

Not good. Because the odds were excellent the next name the teacher read would be mine.

"Werthman," Mr. Hazzard said, pointing a stubby finger at the seat behind Tiffany's.

I managed to stand and move away from the chair without it gripping my hips in a jaws-of-life hold.

For the next twenty minutes, Mr. Hazzard lectured us about the importance of following directions, handing work in on time, and being respectful. I drew squiggly lines with a ball-point pen, thinking about the candy bars in my book bag, the ones Mom had no idea I'd bought before we left Minnesota.

Finally, the bell rang. My tee-shirt brushed against bare skin as I walked, because without the button, the zipper on my jeans splayed open. I had to do something about the jeans. I felt half-dressed. Ducking into a restroom, I locked myself inside the last stall (people didn't tend to notice anybody there) and dug through the zippered side pouch in my book bag. I found a safety pin and pulled the waistband together. With my luck, the pin would pop open and stab me.

Seizing a candy bar, I tore off the wrapper and bit into a huge chunk of chocolate. As I was chewing, I noticed the graffiti on the stall door, scrawled with a black—probably permanent—marker and intended to ruin the reputation of somebody named Alexis A. The smell alone would have driven any normal person out of that stall in a hurry. But not me. I stuffed my face with more bites. There was something seriously wrong with me. Who sits in the john, a dirty, stinky one, and eats chocolate?

The restroom door opened. Purple toenails with white flowers on the big toes came into view. Tiffany. Standing in front of the center sink. She probably needed to spend some quality time with her own reflection. I huddled inside the stall, holding my breath, hoping she wouldn't see it was occupied.

She turned and I thought she was leaving, but instead, she walked toward me, and I hate to admit this, I closed the lid and stepped up onto the toilet seat, so if she peered under the stall, she wouldn't see my feet. The stall door next to mine squealed open and banged shut, and then I heard gagging sounds. Was she sick? On the first day of school? People didn't usually have the stomach flu at the end of summer vacation. Something was off.

The retching sounds continued for a couple of minutes before the toilet flushed. Tiffany crossed to the sinks again. A zipper sound. A click, like a make-up case being opened. Finally, she turned and walked out of the restroom.

Maybe I'd stumbled upon a scandal. Maybe Miss Popular was pregnant. Well, it wasn't any of my business. I was glad she hadn't seen me.

Wadding up the candy wrapper, I lumbered to the sink and washed away the chocolate evidence. I yanked out a handful of paper towels, opened the hinged lid on the trashcan, and dropped the candy wrappers inside.

Out in the hallway, I joined the human current heading for my next class, gym. Even that didn't seem so bad, since a sugar-induced high had kicked in. Weaving through the crowded hallway, I hung a right and…Oh, God, the smell. Chlorine. A swimming pool, behind a glass wall, next to the girls' locker room. All that water. Splashing sounds.

My legs stiffened. I couldn't move. I couldn't bend my knees. Someone was whimpering. Was it me? The floor seemed to float out from under me. The lights were too bright, the white tiles too shiny. I was afraid I'd pass out, or worse, puke. When I tried to scream, the sound died in my throat, the same way it had that day. *Run. Now.*

I turned, too fast, right in the middle of the hallway and collided with someone. My book bag flew out of my hands and landed with a *thunk*. A boy tripped over the bag, a girl bumped into him and fell, causing a three person pile up.

"Hey, loser!" The boy scraped his stuff together and stood.

"What's wrong with you, Lard Butt?" Tiffany, the second human domino.

Clutching my book bag, I struggled to stand and barreled toward the exit at the end of the hallway.

"Freak!" Tiffany's voice sounded far away.

My hands slammed against the door and I rushed outside.

3

The exit opened to a loading dock with a parking lot below it. Too bad the dock wasn't higher, because if it were, I could hurl myself off of it. I was an A+ screw-up. I didn't deserve a second chance. I didn't deserve a life. Why did Dad think things would go back to normal if we moved to another state? No matter how far away we'd moved, my memories were still with me. Truth: There is no escape from yourself.

Holding onto the steel railing beaded with raindrops, I raced down the stairs. At the bottom, a row of dumpsters stood off to the side, overflowing with black garbage bags. I slid down next to the last dumpster, sat on the hard cement. Drawing my knees up, I wrapped my arms around my legs. Rotten food smells wafted in the air. Flies buzzed my face. I swatted them away.

I'd caused a scene in the hallway, and now I was cutting class. Could you get a detention on the first day of school? *Way to go, Lard Butt. Nice first day.*

The boy I'd knocked down in the hallway was right about me. I was a loser. I'd been here, what, an hour? And already I'd made enemies, plus probably half the school had seen the "incident" and now thought I was crazy. Maybe I was.

Any second now, the door would swing open and some teacher would haul me inside and escort me to the principal. Or I'd win a one-way ticket to the school psychologist's office.

Someone pushed the door open, but when I looked up, it wasn't an adult. The WWJD kid scrambled down the steps, his longish brown hair a flyaway mop, the cross necklace fashioned from two silver nails bobbing against his chest. "Are you OK?"

I so did not need this. Me, having a face-off with the Jesus kid. "Could you just leave me alone, please?"

"You're new here, right? I saw what happened."

Hello? Did you not hear me? Go away! I rested my head on my knees.

He crouched next to me, so close I couldn't ignore him because he'd set off my-personal-space-is-being-violated alarm. And then, it happened again, the first degree burn thing warming my face. The I'm-going-to-melt thing. I didn't trust myself to say a word, because there was something about this guy that made me want to spill my guts, like I was sitting in a dark confessional.

"Tiffany's always talking trash about people," he said quietly. "Don't worry about her. I'm Jonah." He shook his long hair back and reached out a hand to me.

I stared at those eyes way too long, and wished I could dive right into them and lose myself forever. Then I looked at his outstretched hand, but I didn't take it. "I'm Lauren. Why are you being so nice? You don't even know me."

Shrugging, he retracted his arm. "We're supposed to be nice to other people."

"Says who?"

He fingered the cross around his neck. "My father."

"Oh, right, God, the all-powerful Being who supposedly wants what's best for all of us." How could

He think death could possibly be what was best for Haley?

He grinned. "Well, Him too, but I meant my dad."

"Leave me alone. I didn't ask for your help, and I don't want it."

"Hey," he held up his hands as if I'd pointed a gun at him, "Just trying to be your friend. Thought you might need one after your hallway debut."

"Funny. You think I planned that?"

Jonah hooked his thumbs into the pockets of his faded blue jeans. "Nah, it was an impromptu performance. You want to talk about it?"

"It's none of your business."

"True, but I think we should go back. Tiffany has a big mouth, and she's probably told somebody by now that you made a break for it."

Right on cue, the door squeaked open. A man wearing a suit and shiny black shoes stepped out onto the loading dock, peering down at us. "What's going on, Jonah? Shouldn't you be in class?"

"The principal," Jonah mouthed to me. "Um, yeah, Mr. Bixby. I was helping a new student find her next class."

Mr. Bixby sighed, ran a hand through his silver hair. "Oh, I see, and her next class is meeting here by the dumpsters?"

"No, sir. I saw Lauren run outside, so I followed her."

"Please tell me you two aren't cutting class."

Jonah smiled. "We're not cutting class."

Mr. Bixby massaged his temple. "If it was anybody else, I wouldn't believe them." He waggled his fingers. "Come on, guys, let's get back inside. I'm sure there's a good explanation for this, but honestly, I already have a killer headache. Miss Vancleave just finished giving me her version of the story."

Jonah shot me an I-told-you-so look before we trailed behind Mr. Bixby, his shoes clicking against the scuff-marked floor. We'd almost reached the end of the hallway before I smelled the chlorine, and I stopped. No way. I wasn't going past the swimming pool.

Mr. Bixby turned. "Lauren?"

Oh, God, the look. The look I'd gotten at the funeral. Mix equal parts of concern and pity and you get the oh-you-poor-kid look. Truth: you can't escape labels from other people.

Jonah stepped toward me. "I'll walk her to the office. We both need passes."

"Not necessary," Mr. Bixby said.

Yeah, so not necessary. Who did this Jesus kid think he was? My personal savior?

Mr. Bixby reached into his suit coat pocket and pulled out a palm-sized pad of paper. He scribbled on the top sheet, tore it off and handed it to Jonah, then wrote one for me. "You know, Lauren, I thought Tiffany was exaggerating when she told me what happened, but now I'm concerned. Perhaps we should call your parents."

"No, I'm fine. Really." I forced a wobbly smile. "It's my first day and I'm nervous, you know?"

My parents couldn't find out about this, especially Mom. She'd have me back in therapy before the end of the week. Therapy stank. The last therapist she dragged me to resembled a Bassett Hound. First thing he did was shove a tissue box at me, like crying was mandatory, and then he expected me to tell him—a total stranger—how I felt. No thank you. I was done with therapy.

"Understandable," Mr. Bixby said, "but you look panicked."

"It's nothing," I said. "The smell of chlorine makes me nauseous."

The principal scratched his head. "Huh, I've never heard that one before."

"Anyway, my parents are at work," I blurted out. "We just moved here, and they both started new jobs today." Mom didn't have a job yet, and Dad didn't go to work at the university until next week. *Thou shalt not lie.* I was heading for Hell, express delivery.

"You're sure you're OK?"

"Yes, absolutely." My lying kicked into auto-pilot, no thinking required.

"All right," Mr. Bixby said. "Then I trust you won't give Miss Vancleave any reason to come running to my office again?"

"I won't," I said.

Mr. Bixby crossed his arms and eyed Jonah and me. "Get to class, both of you."

"Going," Jonah said, grabbing my arm.

"I can walk by myself." I pushed his hand away.

"Uh-huh," he whispered. "I saw how well you did a little while ago."

"Shut up!"

He gripped my arm again, spun me around, and we headed toward the gym hallway.

Chlorine. Splashing. Sweat broke out on my forehead. "I can't go this way."

"Yes you can," Jonah said. "Mr. Bixby is watching. Close your eyes."

"What?"

"Close your eyes," Jonah said, "and hold your breath. I'll guide you."

This was insane, but I had no choice, so I did it.

About a minute later he said, "All clear. You're gonna have to deal with this, you know."

The bell rang. I'd missed the whole gym class. Yes! "Probably, but not today," I said. Jonah stared at me until I merged into the mass of kids moving past us.

"You're welcome!" Jonah shouted.

Traffic was shoulder to shoulder now. Laughter rang out louder than a funhouse soundtrack. I could do this. I could make it through the first day. But what was I going to do tomorrow?

4

The school day finally ended, and I thought my problems were over, at least temporarily, but I was wrong. I hefted myself up the stairs of the bus and scanned the seats for someplace to sit, someplace where I wouldn't draw attention to myself. Too late. Everybody was gawking at me. As I made my way down the center aisle, nobody talked to me, but I was pretty sure people were talking about me. Tiffany had probably texted the entire school about the crazy girl in the hallway. I wished Jonah were here.

Unbelievable. Straight ahead, in the wide back section of the bus, was Tiffany and two other divas-in-training huddled conspiratorially, stealing glances at yours truly. What were the odds we'd have the same bus? Directly in front of Tiffany were the only seats left. Reluctantly, I started to lower myself into a seat, but then Tiffany said, "Those are saved."

Really? Saving seats was against the rules at my old school. "There's no other place to sit."

"So stand." Tiffany sat, smirking, and a chorus of laughter erupted from the diva section.

"No." I sat, turning my back to them.

"Didn't you hear her, freak?" one of Tiffany's friends said. "Those seats are taken."

Turning around, I said, "By whom? Tiffany's imaginary friends?" I was about to say something else when a girl juggling an instrument case, a canvas tote bag, a book bag and a purse tottered along the aisle. Her case and bags bumped other kids' shoulders and legs. "Excuse me," she said. "Sorry."

"Hey, loser," a guy said. "Watch where you're going."

The girl sighed. "I am trying to," she said with a heavy accent. Her skin was the color of milk chocolate, and her black hair snaked down her back in a braid, almost reaching her waist.

"Do you mind if I sit by you?" the girl asked me, lowering herself into the seat before I had a chance to answer her. She smiled, revealing hot pink braces.

Tiffany and company said nothing.

"I am Kavya," she said. "But everyone calls me Jazz because I play trumpet in the Jazz Band."

"I'm Lauren."

Snickering from the diva section. "Hey, look," Tiffany said pointing, "L.B. made friends with Miss Extra-Curricular."

"Brain-challenged," Jazz whispered.

I grinned. "Definitely." L.B.? Oh. Lard Butt. I so wanted to say something about the puking, but the best way to shut someone up was to ignore them. At least that's what my Dad always said.

"Do you play any sports?" Jazz asked.

"Seriously?" Tiffany said. "She can't even walk through the hallway without tripping!"

I hated her. I wanted to humiliate her, make her feel as stupid as I did right then, but I kept quiet. "No, we just moved here from Minnesota."

"I played soccer last year," Jazz said, "and I am trying out for the team again. I also want to join the swim team."

Breathe. So she liked to swim. We could still be

friends.

"Hey, Jazz," Tiffany said, "you should invite L. B. to try out for the swim team too. I heard she loves the swimming pool, don't you, L.B.?"

Did this girl have spies all over the school? How did she hear about my conversation with Mr. Bixby?

Jazz ignored her and turned to me, her eyes shining, as if I was a gift Santa had left under the tree. "You are also a swimmer? The tryouts are soon. Would you like to come with me?"

"I can't." Inhale, exhale.

"Oh. Why not?"

"Because she'll freak!" Tiffany said.

A wave of laughter rippled through the bus, and something broke free inside me. I launched myself out of my seat and grabbed Tiffany by her scrawny arms and shook her. "Why don't you just shut up!"

Tiffany's mascara-enhanced eyes widened. "You're psycho!" she shrieked, trying to push me aside. "Somebody get her off me."

"Awesome," a boy said. "Girl fight."

A group chorus chanted, "Fight, fight, fight." Fists punched the air, like the other kids were cheering on the football team.

"Hey, that's enough!" the bus driver yelled. He hit the brakes, and I stumbled and almost fell. The bus slowed and pulled next to the curb. "Sit down, right now," the driver said.

Strong hands vice-gripped me by the shoulders. Two guys with beefy necks yanked me to the front of the bus, and shoved me into a seat right behind the driver. "Delivery," one guy said, laughing. They both turned and jock-walked down the aisle, then dropped into their seats.

"Stay there," the bus driver ordered, stabbing a pointer finger at me and shooting me a glare.

Heat flooded my cheeks. What had I done? What was wrong with me? I looked over my shoulder. Jazz's mouth hung open. She looked horrified.

"What's your name?" the driver asked.

Oh, God. I'd really done it this time. "Um, Lauren," I whispered.

"Speak up, girl!" the driver said.

"Lauren. Lauren Werthman."

"Well, Miss Werthman, you are in some serious trouble. I'm filing an incident report. Expect to hear from the principal tomorrow morning."

"It wasn't her fault," a voice said from somewhere behind me. I turned. Jazz was standing. "Tiffany was harassing her," she said.

"Yeah, well, sticks and stones," the driver said. "You don't grab somebody for saying stuff about you. Sit down, unless you want to join her in detention." He turned the ignition key, shifted into drive, and hit the gas. The bus lurched forward.

When we reached the next stop, I mumbled, "Sorry" to the bus driver.

"You should be."

Tiffany and company rose from their seats and sashayed forward, each of them shooting me a crusty look as they passed by. Halfway down the steps, Tiffany turned, smiled and said, "Have a nice night, L.B."

There was giggling from the diva gallery, and more kids joined in. I didn't say anything, because that was what she wanted—to goad me, to upset me again. After a few seconds, Miss Popularity stepped down off the bus and the doors whooshed shut behind her.

Leaning back against the seat, I sighed. So every day, this was what I had to look forward to…riding home on the bus with Tiffany and her friends, and listening to their insults.

For the rest of the way home, I rode up front, behind the driver. Finally, we reached my stop. My book bag was still under the seat next to Jazz. Even though I didn't want to, I had to retrieve it. Some kid I didn't even know stuck out his foot as I walked past, but miraculously, I kept my balance. More giggling.

Jazz picked up my bag and held it out to me. "I will talk to Mr. Bixby tomorrow, if you want me to," she said.

"Thanks." I snatched my book bag and trudged to the door.

All the way up my driveway, I called Tiffany every bad name I'd ever heard, but it didn't make me feel any better. I passed Dad's vehicle, and through the garage windows, I saw Mom's car. How was I going to explain my bizarre behavior to them when I didn't even understand it myself?

They'd ground me for life. I was certifiably nuts. I rounded the corner of the house, heading for the back door, because Mom only allowed company to use the front door.

"Lauren!" Dad's voice made me jump. "I've got a surprise for you." He leaned against the cream-colored siding, a flash drive dangling from a cord around his neck, his shirt pocket overflowing with pens. Totally geeky, but I was so glad it was him instead of Mom.

"Hey, Dad." I hoped his surprise was better than mine. Surprise, I got into a fight.

He smiled. Crinkly lines etched the corners of his eyes. "How was your day?"

"OK." I whipped out my best upbeat, no-problems kind of girl expression. I had to tell my parents, but I didn't need to tell Dad right this minute.

"Just OK?"

"It was fine." *Fine.* Except I was the poster child for Murphy's Law...whatever could go wrong, did.

"Good for you, sweetheart. Mom's making dinner."

"Be right there." *Act normal. Look happy.* I slung my book bag over my shoulder and trekked through the door.

Dad followed me into the living room and spread his arms wide. "Ta-Da! Our stuff came today."

Pyramids of boxes, all labeled by Mom, lined the off-white walls.

"Nice," I said, trying to resurrect some enthusiasm.

He dropped his arms to his sides. "Well, I thought you'd be more excited. We have beds too. Don't have to sleep on the floor tonight."

"That's great, Dad. Really." I left him standing, looking baffled, in Box City, and maneuvered through the cardboard maze, following the smell of roasted garlic and chicken. My stomach growled. I hadn't eaten lunch, because I didn't want to show my face in the cafeteria.

The kitchen was wallpapered, with a pattern of miniature pots, pans, and spoons spewed all over it. Seriously ugly. No boxes were stacked against the walls; Mom had unpacked everything in this room. She stood by the countertop, arranging lettuce leaves on plates. Rabbit food, her specialty.

"When's dinner?" I tried not to look up, because I'd caught a glimpse of the plaster cast handprints

Haley and I had made when we were preschoolers. Mine was ten years old, but Haley just made hers last year. They were hanging from lengths of pink ribbon, side by side on the wall opposite the sink.

Mom's forehead furrowed into deeper frown lines. "Five-thirty, same as always."

I cracked the fridge open, perusing the contents: an unopened jar of pickles, salad dressing (low fat), a half-gallon of milk, a dozen eggs, three apples, and Mom's diet cola.

"What are you doing?" she said. "We're going to eat in about two hours. You don't need a snack."

Right. I closed the fridge. I couldn't tell her I hadn't eaten lunch, because then she'd ask why. Slipping past her, I headed for the privacy of my room.

Pausing by the spare bedroom across the hall from mine, I saw it…Haley's Shrine: the dresser from her old room, topped with her pictures from birth to five, and a grouping of her favorite stuffed toys. Mom hadn't unpacked many boxes, but big surprise, Haley's had been one of the first. We'd moved, but here it was, the Past, tagging right along beside us.

After closing my door, I skirted the boxes marked "Lauren's room" and plopped down onto my naked mattress set. Rummaging through my bag, I snatched another crunch bar, ripped the paper off, and jammed the candy into my mouth. Gooey chocolate coated my tongue, and I swallowed the rich flavor, which instantly lifted my mood.

I closed my eyes and slumped against the mattress. In a few minutes, I was dreaming. I knew I was dreaming, because Haley was there.

"Come on, you promised," she whined.

"What?" I said to my best friend, Lexi, pressing

my cellphone tighter against my ear. "Sorry, I didn't hear you. The brat is having a whine fest."

"I'm telling Mom!" Haley said.

"Just a second." I covered the speaker with my hand. "And I'm telling her you don't listen! Go play."

"You said you'd take me."

"I said, maybe. You can wait until Mom and Dad get home."

"You're mean." She wheeled around and stomped out of my room.

"You're mean, you're mean, you're mean..." the words swirled around in my head.

And then Mom's voice, panicky, accusing: "Lauren, where's Haley?"

I shrugged. "In her room."

"No, she's not!" my mother screamed.

I was breathing too fast, gasping for air. My heart pounded in my ears.

"Hey, Lard Butt." Tiffany's voice crashed my dream. "You should have paid attention to your sister."

She didn't know about Haley. How could she?

"You need to deal with this." Jonah materialized next to Tiffany, apparition-style.

I don't want to. Leave me alone!

"Lauren! Dinner's ready." Dad's voice.

Dinner. No Haley. No Tiffany or Jonah. I pushed my sweaty hair away from my face, swung my legs over the side of the bed and trudged toward the garlic smell.

5

I headed for the cupboard to the right of the sink, guessing that was where Mom put the glasses, because she'd kept them there in the old house. The bulging eyes of the frog I'd helped Haley make in ceramics class seemed to follow my every move. She'd painted the frog neon green with yellow stripes, one strange-looking amphibian, and he sat next to the sink gagging on a nylon scrubber. I filled three glasses and set them on the table. Then I pulled out a wooden chair, plopped onto the ruffled cushion, and scooted forward. The table's edge dug into my stomach.

Mom set an orange plate in front of me. She'd already thoughtfully filled it with so-called food: a pile of lettuce topped with vinaigrette, mixed veggies, and half a skinless chicken breast. She and Dad had identical stuff on their plates.

Something was wrong, because Mom still towered over me. "What's smeared around your mouth?" she asked.

If I'd bothered to check a mirror, I could have avoided this inquisition, but I'd stopped looking in mirrors, because I didn't like what I saw. "Nothing." I bowed my head.

She sighed and perched her hands on her hips. "You've been eating in your room again, haven't you? How could you possibly have had time to stock it with junk food already?"

"Let it go," my dad said, taking a bite of chicken. He licked his lips and then his fingers, which drew an ominous glare from Mom. "This is delicious, by the way," he said.

"Tell your father not to change the subject. This is serious." Another wrinkle etched into her forehead.

"You just told him," I said.

"Excuse me?" Mom said.

"Nothing," I mumbled.

"So, are you going to answer me?" she said. "What did you eat? You didn't need a snack before dinner. Especially an empty calorie snack."

Dad dropped his fork, and it clinked against his blue plate. "Just once, could we have a normal meal with normal conversation?"

I stared at the empty chair wedged tight against the table. Haley's chair. Our family was a puzzle missing a piece, incomplete, useless, because you couldn't see the whole picture.

"Obviously your father doesn't care about your health, but I do."

"Classic, Lydia." Dad pushed his plate away. "It's a nice night. I'm eating outside, al fresco. Care to join me, Lauren?" Dad scooted his chair back, piled his silverware on top of his plate, and stood.

He didn't have to ask me twice. I sprang out of my chair.

"We are a family, and we eat together," Mom said, staring at her plate.

"Well, you can come and eat outside with us," Dad said, "and then we'll still be a family."

She didn't join us.

Dad and I sat on the redwood deck, our backs pressed against the house, no chairs, but I didn't care.

A faded-white privacy fence enclosed our large backyard. A light breeze blew. The air smelled clean like freshly washed laundry. The branches on the two maple trees slow danced in the wind.

Dad sipped his diet soda. "Well, the chicken was good, but I gotta say, I'm still hungry." He set his plate on the deck.

I piled my silverware on top of his, dirty dish a la mode, and stacked my plate with his. "Exactly what I was thinking. I already checked the fridge. There's nothing good in there."

He grinned. "I know. I peeked too. Your mom's on a health kick."

Eating outside might actually force Mom to come and get our dishes. The first thing she did after dinner was clean up. She'd put the food away, then load the dishwasher and wipe down the counters and stovetop, although since I started to gain weight, she'd been cooking just enough, so there weren't any leftovers. Tonight, though, she'd just have to throw away the disposable dishes. Our fridge, even at our old house, looked like Mother Hubbard's cupboard.

Dad patted his stomach. "But you know, I don't think I'll starve. So tell me about your school. Did you make any new friends?"

"Well, one. I met a girl named Jazz on the bus. But there's this other girl, Tiffany, and she's a real piece of work." This was my chance. If I told him about the fight, he could talk to Mom for me, and I wouldn't have to tell her.

"Ah, I remember high school. It can be tough. Hey, check it out." He pointed to the driveway. "There's a hoop, and I found the basketball, so how 'bout a game of Horse?"

Waiting to share bad news never improved the situation. I had to tell him. "Yeah, sure. One thing, though, you're probably going to ground me for life after you hear what happened today."

His eyebrows arched up. "This sounds serious. Let's go to my office."

He didn't have an office. Not in this house. I followed him to the garage where he pressed numbers into the keypad. "The code is the date your Mom and I were married."

One garage door squealed open. Dad scooped up the basketball lying on the floor next to the block wall. He bounced the ball a few times and then dribbled it out to the driveway. "OK, kiddo, I'm listening."

"Don't be mad, please?"

He tossed the basketball from hand to hand and twirled it on one finger. "Not making any promises."

"The mean girl I was telling you about? Her name's Tiffany. She was mouthing off during the ride home, and I lost my temper. I sort of pounced on her, which ticked off the bus driver, so he's filing a report, and I'll probably get a detention tomorrow." I rattled off the words fast without taking a breath.

Dad took aim, threw the ball and it slammed into the backboard before dropping through the basket. "Your shot."

"Did you hear what I said?"

"Yep. I just don't know what to say, Lauren. I'm trying to understand why you'd pounce on somebody just because they teased you. Take your shot."

I dribbled, aimed, and let the ball roll off my fingertips. Swish, it dropped through the net. "There's more."

"I figured."

Facing away from the hoop, I heaved the ball over my head and then heard the satisfying sound again of ball meeting net.

Dad dribbled a few times and stared at the hoop (as if that would help) before he turned his back on it. With a two-handed launch, the ball flew over his head, hit the rim and careened into the street. "I have an H," he said, jogging to catch the runaway ball.

When he returned, he draped his arm across my shoulders and steered me to the deck. "Intermission. Want a soda?"

I nodded. He disappeared through the sliding glass door and came back holding two diet colas. We popped the tabs in sync, as if we'd rehearsed it. I took a cold, bubbly drink, and a strong chocolate craving hit me. I still had some crunch bars left in my book bag, unless Mom had gone on a search and seizure and destroyed them.

Dad wiped his mouth on his sleeve. "You gave me the condensed version, now I want the whole story, every dirty detail."

I told him everything, starting with me freaking out in the hallway near the pool, and he never interrupted, just listened and nodded his head.

Across the street, a leaf-blower whirred on, and a guy cleared grass clippings from his sidewalk and driveway. Two boys about my age streaked past our house, riding dirt bikes way too small for them.

The sun baked down on us. I shielded my eyes, squinting at Dad. "So, do you think I'm crazy? Because I'm starting to think I am."

"Nope. Crazy people never wonder whether there might be something wrong with them. And I'm not going to ground you."

"Seriously?"

"Seriously. But, kiddo, we need to get you some help."

"No! I'm not going to another stupid therapist." Moving away from Minnesota didn't change anything. All the bad stuff had followed me here.

"Honey, listen, you're still dealing with a lot, and I think it would help you to talk to somebody about it."

"I can talk to you." I used my whiny voice and pouted, along with a generous scoop of pleading-- things that always made Dad cave when I was younger.

He frowned and crossed his arms. "I'm not qualified, and besides, I'm too close to the situation. I'm part of it."

"Do you have to tell Mom?"

"No, I don't have to tell her. You do."

"Dad, come on!"

"Tell me what?" Mom stood by the open screen door. Wispy strands of hair hung in her eyes; dark circles discolored the skin underneath them. She stepped onto the deck.

"Lauren had a problem today," Dad said, "and she needs to explain to you what happened."

"Great, just what we need, another problem." Mom stooped to grab the dishes.

That was what I'd become to her: one big, fat problem. Haley never caused problems. She never got in trouble. She was the good daughter. And now Mom was stuck with me.

Mom didn't seem surprised about my meltdown by the pool, but she was surprised when I told her I'd practically attacked Tiffany. All she said was "Lauren…" but it was the way she said it, in an "I-am-so-tired-of-this" voice, a "how-could-you-do-that?" voice, that made me realize I'd disappointed her again. Story of my life.

"Well," Mom said, "apparently you quit going to therapy too soon."

Dad nodded his agreement.

I hate it when parents gang up on you and present a united front, because then you know you are doomed, and there is no way you can get out of whatever they've decided. The only thing in my favor was, it would take Mom some time to find a therapist in Nebraska.

"I'll call your school tomorrow," Mom said. "I think I read online the school has a psychologist on staff."

Great. So much for that theory.

6

The next morning, a summons arrived for me from Principal Bixby. I was to report to his office immediately. I expected it, yes, but still, I was hoping for a miracle, like the incident report would just go poof and disappear.

Mr. Bixby's secretary had clown-orange hair pulled tight against her head and drawn into a bun in back. I handed her my note. "Have a seat, Lauren," Mrs. Burns said. "Mr. Bixby will be with you in a minute."

A long counter separated the waiting area, where I stood, from the work area, where a row of desks ran parallel to the counter. Black file cabinets flanked the wall behind the desks. Fluorescent tube lights shined through plastic panels in the ceiling, making Mrs. Burns's skin look pasty white, almost translucent. Grayish veins branched out under the flesh on her hands.

Everything in the room was colorless and cold. The counter was the dividing line between students and staff. If you crossed the line, it usually meant you were in trouble.

Fish wriggled through the water in the aquarium on the wall next to me. Pink rock lined the bottom, and green plants fluttered against a gold-brown castle. A silver lid topped the aquarium. This water didn't make me want to run screaming from the room, because really, how could anyone drown in it? It was contained, and the fish knew how to swim.

Mrs. Burns tap-tap-tapped on her keyboard and glanced at a piece of paper beside her computer. The phone rang and she picked it up and said, "Good morning, Evington Heights High School. How may I help you? I'll transfer you. Please hold."

Mr. Bixby appeared, striding through the doorway of an inner-office, wearing a crisply pressed shirt and a red tie knotted at his neck. In his hand, he carried a typewritten paper. The report the bus driver filed?

He walked around the counter and stood in front of me. "Lauren Werthman?" He pointed at me, shaking his finger a few times as if he were trying to remember. "Oh, you're that friend of Jonah's who was out by the dumpsters yesterday, right? I thought your name looked familiar."

I was not a friend of Jonah's, but from what I saw, Mr. Bixby liked Jonah, so I nodded and swallowed my protest.

"Well, come with me," Mr. Bixby said. "Let's try to figure out what we're going to do about this." He flicked two fingers against the report.

His office had an L-shaped desk, clutter free, with a flat-screened computer monitor on top. Stacked filing boxes held neat piles of papers. A silver-framed photo of a woman and a boy wearing a soccer uniform sat next to the computer. Mr. Bixby was somebody's dad.

Two straight-backed chairs faced the desk. He motioned for me to sit, and he sat in the leather chair behind the desk like a judge taking the bench, ready to sentence the defendant. "First of all," he said, "you should know I talked with both your parents this morning, and they are very concerned about you, as am I." He reclined slightly in his chair and laced his fingers behind his head, studying me as if I were some kind of rare specimen in a petri dish.

This was what I hated about being a minor: Not being allowed to make my own decisions. An adult, or multiple adults in my case, could decide my fate, and I didn't get a vote. I kept quiet, waiting for him to tell me more, pretty sure I wouldn't like it.

Principal Bixby cleared his throat. "Your parents told me about your sister's accident. I'm very sorry."

They'd promised! They swore they wouldn't tell anybody at my new school about Haley, because I begged them not to. I clenched my hands into tight fists. It was Mom. Dad wouldn't break his promise. How was I supposed to start with a clean slate now that the principal knew all the baggage I was lugging around? I'd get the pity look from him and every teacher he shared the information with.

"Thanks," I whispered.

His expression stayed in serious mode as he went on. "Your reaction in the hallway makes a whole lot more sense to me now," he said. "But you do realize you were out of line on the bus, don't you?"

"What about Tiffany?"

"I know Miss Vancleave is not blameless, but we're talking about your behavior now, not hers. You physically attacked her, and I can't ignore that."

It wasn't like I hurt her. She didn't have any bruises. But actions have consequences.

"I'm afraid I have to give you a detention. Today. I can't condone fighting. Your dad said he could come and get you afterwards."

I nodded slowly, even though this was totally unfair. On a scale of one to ten, ten being the best, I'd already decided to rate this day a two, and I'd only been to one class.

Leaning forward in his chair with, oh, God, here it came, the Bassett Hound expression, Mr. Bixby said, "We're here to help, Lauren. Me. All your teachers. We want you to feel comfortable at Evington Heights."

He thought I'd feel comfortable serving a detention?

Mrs. Burns leaned inside the doorway. "Excuse me, Mr. Bixby? There were two students here earlier, and they wrote notes and said it was urgent you read them." She crossed to the desk and laid folded pieces of notebook paper in front of him.

"Thank you. I will read them as soon as I'm finished talking to Miss Werthman."

Mrs. Burns pivoted on her sensible-heeled shoes, reached the doorway, and turned. The ends of her glasses were shackled to a chain around her neck, and she had a pencil tucked behind one ear. She knocked lightly on the door frame.

"Something else?" Mr. Bixby asked.

"I'm sorry to interrupt you, sir, but the students said you should read the notes right away, because they concern Miss Werthman."

"All right. Thank you."

"Yes, sir." Mrs. Burns returned to her own desk, typing on her keyboard, but every few minutes, she glanced toward Mr. Bixby's door, and I knew she was eavesdropping.

Mr. Bixby straightened in his chair and unfolded one note, his eyes scanning the page. When he finished, he snatched the other note, read it, and leaned back in his chair, eyeing me suspiciously, as if I were a co-conspirator in an ingenious plot to overthrow the system. This interruption wasn't my doing.

"Kavya Krishnan and Jonah Prescott wrote the notes," he said, "if you didn't already know."

I shook my head. Jazz had told me she'd speak to the principal on my behalf, but Jonah? Did they know each other? This was the first time I'd heard their last names. They hardly knew me, yet they'd written Mr. Bixby, presumably to tell him I was not responsible for the trouble yesterday.

"Well," Mr. Bixby said, clearing his throat, "you seem to have made friends already. It is their opinion what transpired yesterday was not your fault."

Maybe he wouldn't give me a detention. Maybe he'd hand me a get-out-of-jail-free card this time and let me off with a warning, thanks to Jazz and Jonah. "It wasn't."

Folding his hands, Mr. Bixby sighed. "Jonah and Kavya are two of our best students, and I respect their opinions, but it still doesn't change the facts. You acted inappropriately. If I make an exception in this case, it will set a precedent, and every young person in this school will expect me to bend the rules."

So it didn't matter that it wasn't my fault? It didn't matter that witnesses said Tiffany had started it? Foul! Nothing would happen to Tiffany. There were no consequences for her inappropriate behavior.

"Look, for what it's worth," Mr. Bixby said, "I wish I didn't have to follow through with this, but I do. So, you'll report to Mr. Hazzard, Room 201, after the last bell."

Mr. Hazzard? My unsmiling history teacher? How many kids besides me were dumb enough to get a detention on the first day of school? Maybe I'd be the only one there. "Can I go now?"

"One more thing. When I spoke to your mother this morning, I mentioned we have an excellent psychologist right here at our school. Your mom and I both agreed seeing Miss Gladden would be a step in the right direction for you. How do you feel about that?"

I shrugged. What did he expect me to say? All right! Another therapist. I can't wait! Mr. Bixby was another adult pushing me into something I didn't want to do, but I had no choice.

He reached for his phone and pushed a button. "Miss Gladden?" he said, glancing up at me. "Would you be able to see a student second period today? Lauren Werthman." Mr. Bixby nodded. "Thank you so much."

Today. As in, this is an emergency. I've got a broken kid here, and you need to fix her. I'd been judged and sentenced, just like that. No plea bargaining, no parole.

"Well, you're in luck, Lauren. She can squeeze you in. Her office is two doors down from mine."

Lucky me. I thanked him, which seemed dumb under the circumstances, and then I lifted my backpack off the floor and shuffled out of his office.

I understood why he gave me the detention, he was just doing his job, but I still resented him for siding with my parents and forcing me to see Miss Gladden.

It hit me after I returned to my first period class: I was meeting with the school psychologist second period, the same time I was supposed to go to gym. Coincidence? No way.

7

When I knocked on Miss Gladden's door, a voice said, "Come." Not "Come in," like a normal person would say.

I pushed open the door. Seated behind a chrome and glass desk, listening via an ear bud wired to an MP3 player, was a woman who looked like she could pass for a student. A butterfly tattoo peeked from under one purple shirt sleeve. Her blonde hair was braided in corn rows, and the braids hung well past her shoulders.

She removed the ear bud and took a sip of hot chocolate from a steaming mug that read, "Life is short. Eat dessert first."

"You must be Lauren," she said, setting down the mug. "I'm Miss Gladden. I know, bizarre name for a school psychologist, right? You can call me Candra, if you'd like." She smiled as if we'd been friends since forever.

The walls were painted a lime green, not a trace of the boring off-white that dominated the rest of the office area. White mini blinds clothed the windows. Leafy tendrils spilled over the sides of potted plants. On a credenza, behind her desk, was a metal cage, and a hamster sprinted on a squeaky wheel.

Miss Gladden, Candra, noticed me watching the hamster. "Lauren, meet Harley. Harley, Lauren."

The hamster paused long enough to twitch its

whiskers at me before he resumed running in a circle, covering distance but getting nowhere. Kind of like me and my life.

I felt like Dorothy in *The Wizard of Oz* when she entered the wizard's chamber. What would Miss Gladden expect from me? How could I pass her evaluation and get off the parental radar?

"So," Candra said, rising and pointing to two chairs parked on a shag rug, "Sit."

Come. Sit. What was next, speak? Did she treat everybody like a dog in obedience training or just me? Whatever. Being here was better than gym where I could smell the swimming pool.

I plopped into a chair and she dropped into the other. Thankfully, when I met her stare, there was no pity in her eyes, and not even a touch of Bassett Hound. She was more like a Golden Retriever, devoted and loyal and completely tuned into me. She wasn't sizing me up, she wasn't doing triage on a broken kid like all the other doctors had done. Instead, she was sitting there with an expectant look on her face, like she really wanted to hear whatever I had to say, like a faithful pet who loves you unconditionally. Dad looked at me the same way sometimes when he wasn't too busy, but Mom never did. Not anymore.

"Tell me why you're here," she said, tucking a long braid behind one triple-pierced ear.

She didn't know? I figured it was front page news at Evington Heights. I was sure Tiffany had gotten the exclusive and reported it to the whole school by now. I mean how many psycho kids walked these halls? "Um, Principal Bixby sent me."

"I know, but why?"

"I guess I have issues...mostly one big issue."

Candra pulled her legs up onto the chair, wrapped her arms around them and rested her chin on her knees. "Speak."

There it was. I had to stifle a grin. And why was she sitting with her feet on the chair? Adults weren't supposed to sit in chairs that way. My mother would have a fit if I were wearing boots like Candra and didn't kick them off before I put my feet on the furniture.

"My sister, Haley." I'd avoided saying her name out loud, because it hurt. I couldn't even remember the last time I'd said it. My hands felt shaky and sweaty. Tears welled in my eyes and I blinked, trying to get them to go away so they wouldn't spill down my face. I had to stay strong for what was coming next, when she told me she knew about Haley and offered her sympathy. Sympathy didn't help me. It only reminded me I didn't deserve to have other people feel sorry for me, and it kept me wallowing in self-pity and guilt.

"So, what? You don't get along with your sister?"

Principal Bixby hadn't told her anything? My mouth felt like I'd eaten a sleeve of soda crackers. I stared at my lap and slowly shook my head.

"Well, it's pretty normal not to get along with siblings."

The hamster's treadmill squeaked as he raced around and around, faster and faster. The squealing grew louder until I wanted to scream at him to stop.

"I don't fight with my sister anymore," I mumbled.

Candra was trying to categorize me, find out which group I fit into. She must talk to a lot of kids who had problems with siblings. Funny how I used to think Haley was my major problem, how often I'd thought she was a pain in the butt. I'd even wished I didn't have a sister. It's true...be careful what you wish for.

"That's good."

"No, it's not. Haley's..." The word stuck in my mouth. I didn't want to say dead because being dead is so final, as if you've never lived at all. I didn't want to see pity in Candra's eyes or worse, shock.

"Haley's what? You can tell me, Lauren. I won't share it with anyone else."

A bead of sweat snaked down my back. My heart jack-hammered against my chest. I glanced at the clear acrylic clock on the wall. The second hand crawled past the numbers on the clock face, tick, tick, tick. I'd been in her office for thirty minutes. Second period would last another hour.

"I don't want to talk about it." Unacceptable, I knew. She'd keep battering me with questions until I had to answer her just so she'd leave me alone. This was the way it worked with doctors.

"Fair enough. What do you want to talk about?"

Huh? This had never happened before. Not with the Bassett Hound. Not with the other lady I saw before him. "Nothing," I mumbled.

Candra's boots hit the rug as she sprang out of her chair. "Fine. Would you like a cup of hot chocolate?"

Fine? "Sure."

"Good." A mini microwave sat on a small glass-topped table in the corner. Crossing the room, she grabbed an instant hot chocolate envelope from a dish on top of the microwave. She poured water from a pitcher into a mug that read, "I hate Mondays" and popped the mug into the microwave. A minute later, she removed the mug, tore open the packet, and dumped the powdered mix into the cup, stirring it with a plastic spoon. She walked back to me. "Here you go."

"Thanks."

"No problem. You'll be meeting with me for a while, Lauren. Second period. And I hope you'll want to share what's going on in your life, but it's totally up to you what we talk about."

"Seriously?" How long was a while? Did I ever have to go to gym?

"Yep. We don't have to discuss anything that makes you feel uncomfortable, unless you want to."

There had to be a catch. There was always a catch. If it sounded too good to be true and all that.

Candra's gaze swiveled toward the clock. "We have another forty-five minutes. Let's get to know one another, OK?"

Trap ahead. I had heard this line before. "I guess."

"Let's tell each other three things we like to do. I'll start."

She'd start? My discussions with other therapists had all been pretty much one-sided. They asked the questions and I was supposed to answer them.

Tucking her legs up onto the chair again, she sipped her hot chocolate, and then set the mug on the lamp table between our chairs. Without a coaster. I could just hear my mother...

"Here goes. I like to ride my motorcycle. Guess what kind I have?"

A shrink who rode a motorcycle? And worked for the public school system? "A Harley?"

"Ding, ding, ding." She clapped her hands. "Here's another one. I like to spend time on my computer. Guess what my favorite thing to do is?"

This was no ordinary adult. "Um, Facebook?"

"Ah, you're good, but specifically what activities on Facebook? And by the way, if you have an account, friend me and we can chat online. Then you'll always know you can reach me. I want to give you my cell number, too." She snatched a business card from the small silver holder on the table, turned it over, scribbled a number on it, and passed it to me.

"Thank you." If I believed in God, which was a big if, I might have thought Candra was somebody sent by Him to do an intervention in my life. Sure, the other doctors had given me their phone numbers. Their office numbers. And I could call during business hours. Yes, there was somebody on call for emergency situations, but not everyday problems.

"What's the third thing I like to do?" she asked.

It could have been anything. Skydiving? "I give up."

"I volunteer at the homeless shelter once a week. Usually on Saturdays. When I was eight years old, my mother and I were homeless, living in our car. Your turn."

"You really lived in your car?"

"Yep. We lived in Missouri then, and it was summer. By the time winter rolled around, my mom had found a better paying job, and we rented a dinky apartment. I could tell you lots of stories. Oh, no fair. You were supposed to share something about yourself."

Me? I didn't do much of anything anymore. Not since Haley died. I mean, how was I supposed to enjoy any activity after losing my little sister? "I don't know what to say."

"Oh, come on. You must like to do something. Or

maybe it's something you used to enjoy, but for whatever reason, you stopped doing it."

"I used to play soccer," I blurted out. She was good.

"There you go! You could join the girls' team here."

"No, I couldn't. I've gained like fifty pounds."

"So? Get back in shape. You can do it. What else?"

"I played clarinet in the band at my old school."

"Awesome. Well, our time's almost up, Lauren, but I want you to do something for me. Every day."

This couldn't be good. "What?"

"Hang on." She walked to her desk, opened a lower side drawer and retrieved a spiral notebook. "From now on, this is your journal. I want you to write in it every day, even if it's only one sentence. Even if it's a sentence like, 'today sucked.' The idea is to get your feelings down on paper, to let them out. You don't have to show me or anyone else what you've written, but you might want to talk about it sometimes. Deal?"

It didn't sound too tough. One sentence a day. "OK."

She walked over to me, laid the notebook in my lap, and extended her hand. "It was nice to meet you, Lauren. I'm looking forward to seeing you tomorrow. Same time, same place."

I was looking forward to meeting with her again too. She was different, not like any other doctor I'd known. The bell rang. "Well, bye."

"Bye."

Dodging kids in the hallway, I actually believed I might have a shot at a normal life again.

Until Tiffany raged up to me and said, "Thanks a

lot, Lard Butt. I got a detention because of you!"

8

"Reject!" Tiffany's flawless, magazine model face was inches from mine. I smelled mints on her breath. "Why'd you tell Mr. Bixby the fight was my fault, when you were the one who attacked me? Huh?" Her eyes glowed like a fire reduced to hot coals. I waited for her head to spin.

Passing period was only three minutes long. Since we'd already used up some of the time, I figured Tiffany couldn't kill me in under three minutes. Some kids stopped to watch, like people who rubberneck at a car accident. Apparently, it's fascinating to view carnage, even impending carnage.

"Leave her alone," Jonah said, wedging himself between us.

Tiffany spun to face him. "Go away, freak. This isn't any of your business."

"Lauren didn't tell Mr. Bixby anything. I did."

"You weren't on the bus," Tiffany said.

But then she had a thought-bubble moment, just like a cartoon character in the comic strips. Her brain reminded me of an abandoned warehouse, plenty of room for storage, but empty.

"Jazz told you, didn't she? I forgot you two were like this." Tiffany crossed her fingers, held them in front of his face and smiled at him. "But I didn't know you and Miss Extra Curricular were friends with L.B."

"My name's Lauren." I so wanted to slap her.

"L.B.?" Jonah said.

"Just a nickname," Tiffany said.

"Don't ask," I told him.

Tiffany reached out and held Jonah's cross necklace against the palm of her hand, and then let it slip off and come to rest against his chest. "So, let me guess, you heard me picking on your fat girlfriend here, and you, being Saint Jonah, had to swoop in and defend her, right?"

Color washed over Jonah's face, sunburn red, and I was afraid he was going to shove her or even hit her, but he stood still. Mt. St. Jonah, ready to explode. He glared at Tiffany like a pit bull ready to pounce.

Girlfriend? "I'm not his girlfriend!"

Stunned expressions played across every face in the hallway. I could hear the rumors circulating through school: Guess what? The girl who freaked out by the pool is the Jesus kid's girlfriend. Can you believe it? Another lie spread by Tiffany. The girl was evil, and I had to stop her. Even Jonah couldn't dispute my "eye for an eye" mentality. I'd read it in the Bible once, during Mom's religious phase. "Families that go to church together, stay together," she used to tell us. I'd had doubts all along about there being a God, but Haley's death was the deal breaker for me. There was no God, no Higher Being looking out for us. Why would a loving God let my sister die?

"What's the matter with you?" Tiffany said, tightening the screws in Jonah's frayed temper. "Got nothing to say? Oh, I get it, it's that turn-the-other-cheek-thing, right? God, you're so weird."

"Come on," I said to Jonah, tugging on his arm much the same way as he'd done to lead me out of the hallway by the swimming pool. "Let's go."

Jonah's posture stiffened. His hands balled into fists. His breathing quickened. "Leave God out of this," he said evenly. He might have turned the other cheek, but both of his were reddening now.

"Hey," I yelled, looking straight at Tiffany. "Have you hugged a toilet today?"

More kids in the hall paused to listen. Jaws dropped.

"What did you say?" Tiffany spit out the words.

Jonah was staring at me.

So was everybody else who'd gathered around us.

"I said, have you thrown up today? I heard you. Gagging and puking in the restroom. And you kept doing it." I shouldn't have said it, but she had it coming—for all the name calling, and for picking on Jonah and Jazz.

"What, were you spying on me, you freak?" she screamed. Her face flushed as her miniscule brain tried to think up a better come back. "You are soooo dead!"

I pulled Jonah's arm again and this time he followed me. Walking side by side, we left Tiffany standing there, a series of four-letter expletives pelting us in the back.

I didn't even turn around. Now she knew how I felt. Embarrassed. Humiliated. But at what cost? Tiffany knew I'd seen her throwing up, but had it happened more than once? And if she'd had a stomach virus, then she would have said something, wouldn't she? Right now, there was a fifty-fifty chance kids were gossiping about her instead of me. I'd definitely started something here. I'd declared war with the most popular girl in the ninth grade. I was dead.

Jonah took long strides up the hallway, a deep frown chiseled on his face. I had to jog just to keep up with him. A few seconds later, he stopped, leaned against the wall, folded his hands and closed his eyes. His lips moved, but he didn't say anything, as if he were lip-syncing the words to a song.

Really? He was praying? Right here in the middle of the school hallway? No wonder kids thought he was weird. He talked to himself. Because nobody was listening…I knew that for a fact.

I touched his shirtsleeve. "We're going to be late."

"Shhh." He mouthed more words. Finally, he opened his eyes. "I was asking God to help me control my temper."

"Great. Can't you talk to Him in private?"

The redness faded from his face. His breathing steadied. "I'm not ashamed to pray in public."

"Well, it made me feel really uncomfortable."

For a second, I thought I'd made him mad. He squinted at me, as if I was some alien life-form, but then he took a deep breath and shook his head.

Wisps of long, brown hair fell over his eyes, eyes so clear and blue I could have dived into them, and he touched my arm. Electricity passed from his fingertips clear through my skin. "So you're not my girlfriend, huh? Guess I'll have to settle for the friend part."

In slow motion, he leaned toward me, resting both his hands on my shoulders now. My legs got all wobbly and my stomach felt warm and fluttery. He was going to kiss me. In front of everybody! And the weirdest thing was, I wanted him to.

"Brrrrring!" the bell rang, and we both flinched. He backed away from me. "Well, I guess we'd better go," he said in a low voice. Frowning he said, "Why'd you say that to Tiffany? Maybe she ate something and it made her sick."

"Maybe, but I don't think so." I stared at the cross he always wore. He really believed there was a God, but if there was, I'd have to hate Him for not keeping Haley safe. "Oh, thanks for sending Mr. Bixby the note. Tiffany got a detention."

Jonah smiled. "Well that explains her verbal assault. You just made things worse, you know."

"Yeah, I know, but she shouldn't have said those things to you. And by the way, Mr. Bixby gave me a detention too."

"Oh, sorry. Just when I was starting to think he was OK. Jazz and I tried to explain what happened on the bus wasn't your fault."

"I heard. Thanks." We walked until we reached the end of the hallway.

His long fingers curled over my hand. My palm got all sweaty. My heart crashed like a bird hitting a glass pane.

"Something I wanted to ask you," he said.

Ask me anything. I'll say yes. He was going to ask me out. He was going to tell me he wanted to be more than just friends. "Go ahead."

"What were you doing in Miss Gladden's office? Is she helping you with your phobia?"

Jerking my hand free, I practically ran away from him. That's the trouble with friends. They think it's OK to pry and ask personal questions. I stormed off in the other direction. I didn't need any friends. I'd go it alone.

The rest of the day was uneventful, dull even, thank goodness. I collected the books I needed from my locker and marched off to serve my sentence in detention.

9

Room 201 was an interior room, a windowless cell with gray tables and folding chairs. Standing in the front of the room was my history teacher, Mr. Hazzard, scowling, definitive lines etched into his chin as if it were hinged like a marionette's. His marble green eyes were glazed over, like he'd seen enough trouble today and didn't care to see me, another misfit, file into the room for detention.

"You're late, Miss Werthman," he barked.

"Sorry. I couldn't get my locker open." *Thou shalt not lie...* Why did these verses pop into my head at exactly the wrong moment?

"Uh-huh," he said with obvious sarcasm. He gestured with a hairy arm. "Please sit down."

A guy with a pierced tongue—I saw it when he yawned—slouched in the back row. He had an eyebrow ring and a lip ring too. Snake and vine tattoos covered both arms. A girl smacking gum sat next to him. She wore a spaghetti-strapped top that looked like lingerie, a skirt so short it belonged in a figure skater's wardrobe, and a smirk that screamed, "I have attitude."

Another guy, whose eyes were closed—as if this experience was too boring to even be present—reeked of smoke. He wore jeans with holes ripped strategically up and down both legs and a black tee-shirt that read, "Life Sucks and Then You Die."

What am I doing here? I didn't belong with these kids. Four of us, including me, but no Tiffany or Jonah. I didn't really expect Jonah to come though. Not after I'd yelled at him. Besides, he could charm his way out of detention. Mr. Bixby liked him, so my guess was most of the teachers did too.

I'd wondered how many kids were dumb enough to get a detention the second day of school and now I had my answer: There was no shortage of stupidity at Evington Heights.

"OK, people," Mr. Hazzard said, "here are the rules in detention. You may not sleep, read, eat, converse, use your cellphone, or anything else that might save you from mind-numbing boredom for the next hour. The two allowable activities are sitting and breathing. Go!" He clapped his hands.

Those of us standing scattered like mice and found seats.

B.O. wafted through the stuffy room, most of it coming from Pierced-Tongue Guy, who probably hadn't touched soap in this decade.

After a few minutes, Lingerie Girl's eyes fluttered shut.

It took exactly two seconds for Mr. Hazzard's reaction. "You!" he barked. "Open your eyes. Now!"

"Whatever," she said, pulling up one spaghetti strap that had looped over her pale shoulder.

"In my room, young lady, you will treat me with respect." Mr. Hazzard slammed a pencil and a lined piece of paper down on the table in front of her. "I want you to write 200 times, 'I will not respond flippantly to a teacher.' Oh, and write the definition of flippantly at the top of the page. If you don't know what it means, there's a dictionary on the corner of my desk. Look it up!"

"What?" Her lip-glossed mouth hung open in an "O" shape.

"You heard me."

OK, then. The rest of us sat like stone-chiseled statues.

Ten minutes later, Tiffany strolled into the room, as if she was walking through the mall window shopping.

"Miss Vancleave," Mr. Hazzard said. "So nice of you to join us."

Tiffany finger-combed her hair, and then there was the unmistakable sound of a cellphone signaling an incoming text message.

Uh-oh.

She unzipped her purse and reached inside, pulling out her cellphone, and her thumbs worked the keys. All eyes swiveled toward Mr. Hazzard.

"Miss Vancleave, this is not a chat room," he bellowed. "Put it away."

"Um, just a sec." Her thumbs continued to hit the keys.

"When I ask you to do something," Mr. Hazzard said, propping his hands on his hips, "I don't mean in a sec."

"Ooookaaaay." Tiffany dropped the phone back into her purse.

"And if you hadn't been ten minutes late getting here," he went on, "you would have known using a cellphone in here is against my rules."

She actually smiled a what-a-jerk smile, and then she looked at us, like she was seeking confirmation.

No way.

"Miss Vancleave," Mr. Hazzard said in a too quiet

voice, "I do believe you'd benefit from sharing my company again tomorrow after school for a second detention."

"What? That's not fair!" Tiffany said.

Mr. Hazzard sighed. "Life's not fair," he said as if he were explaining something to a preschooler. "Get used to it."

Yes!

"What are you smiling about?" Mr. Hazzard strolled toward me. His old-man, scroll-punched dress shoes squeaked with each step. He stopped next to my chair and glared down at me.

Was I smiling? I didn't even realize it. It just happened.

"Well? You gonna answer me in this lifetime? What's so humorous, Miss Werthman?"

"Nothing." I felt my smile flat-line.

The clock on the wall whispered a steady rhythm as the second hand crawled past each number. Forty-five minutes to go in the hour long detention.

"Nothing? Gee, that's not very funny." He looked around the room. "Do you guys think that's funny?"

"Kinda." Lingerie Girl giggled.

"Yeah, you would." Mr. Hazzard did an eye roll.

There was giggling in unison now, as if somebody had held up the laughter cue card in front of a live audience.

Truth: In high school, there is nothing worse than being targeted by a sadistic teacher who would probably like nothing better than to see you humiliated. Unless there are a bunch of juvenile delinquents watching the drama unfold, and you are all sharing a cramped, smelly room with absolutely no air circulation.

Sweat pooled under my armpits. My lower lip quivered. Two more minutes passed.

"All right, Miss Werthman. Here's what we'll do since you can't answer my question. As you know, I am a history teacher by day. Overseeing detention is only a part-time gig."

There was more snickering from the live audience.

"First thing tomorrow morning," he said, "I want a five-hundred word essay from you on a prominent historical figure, and it better be good. If I do not receive said essay, you will report to me after school for a second detention. Are we clear?"

Yes, sergeant, yes sir! "Yes." I skipped the salute. A five-hundred word essay on a prominent person. This was absurdity at its finest. But if I didn't write it, I'd land in Hazzardville again with Tiffany.

He glanced at the clock. "OK, people, if I were you, I wouldn't bother me again." He waddled—yes waddled from side to side because he was so overweight—to the desk in the front of the room, sank into the chair, propped his feet up, and then cracked open a book.

Even Tiffany kept her mouth shut, but she cast dirty looks at me at regular intervals.

Periodically, Mr. Hazzard's gaze turned toward the clock. When the hour was finally up, he said, "You are dismissed. Please don't come back. Except you, Miss Vancleave. I will see you tomorrow. And you, Miss Werthman, with essay in hand. If you bring donuts, I prefer glazed, and I like hazelnut coffee. I take it black."

I wasn't at all sure he was kidding about the donuts and coffee until he gave me a Grinchy grin. I grabbed my bag and shot out of Room 201 as quick as an athlete on steroids, before Tiffany had a chance to run off at the mouth again, because I knew she wasn't done tormenting me.

10

I speed-walked to the school's front entrance, and pushed open the glass door, hustling outside into the hot, sticky air. Heat waves shimmered above the cement. The flowers planted around the flagpole had brown-tinged leaves and dried buds. Cracks split the soil in a few bare spots on the lawn. The predicted high for today was ninety-five.

Kids clustered near the building, some in groups, some alone, texting, and chatting with friends. Buses were parked parallel to the school in the bus zone, waiting to carry kids who had after school activities home. After school activities like detention. Was Tiffany catching a bus ride home? Thank God, Dad was picking me up.

Thank God? Just an expression.

Dad's truck wasn't parked in the front lot, so I walked to the side one, but he wasn't there either. Where was he?

"Hey!" Tiffany yelled from somewhere behind me. "Where do you think you're going?"

Um, home. I just wanted to go home. What was her problem? It wasn't my fault she showed up late for detention and broke Mr. Hazzard's rules, or that I'd heard her puking, but apparently, in Tiffanyland, whenever things went wrong, you blamed somebody else. I didn't think she'd actually kill me, but would she beat me up? Yeah, probably, if she got the chance.

Out of breath, sure she was chasing me, I veered around the corner of the building and yanked on a side door. Miraculously, it was unlocked, so I ducked inside the first open door I came to. Adrenaline pulsed through my body. Somebody coughed and I realized I wasn't alone.

Sitting at a table near the back of the classroom, a skinny kid, pencil poised over an open sketchpad, looked up at me with questioning, pea-green eyes. I raised a finger to my lips to shush him and stood with my back flat against the wall next to the door. Tiffany could peer in at any second, and I couldn't take another battle today.

"W-W-We in lockdown or something?" the kid said. He grinned, and you could have shoved three playing cards in the gap between his teeth. Greasy black hair, parted in the middle, covered half of both eyes. A pimple population had exploded on his forehead. His tee-shirt was a faded, tie-dyed green with a giant white peace symbol across the front. He looked like a retro kid whose parents were former hippies and drove around in a VW wagon plastered with bumper stickers that said things like, "Send our kids to college not war" and "Give peace a chance."

"No," I whispered. "Can you just act like I'm not here?"

His thin lips twitched, he shrugged and once again glided the pencil across the paper.

Easels stood at attention in even rows with blank canvases propped against them. Splattered with color, the easels held tubes of paint in their trays. An art classroom.

I waited maybe ten minutes before I checked the hallway. A janitor pushed a wide dust mop up and down the length of the hall. Gray metal lockers stood soundlessly on the sidelines. Two teachers talked in front of a backlit display case with framed photos and trophies. No Tiffany. Closing the door, I turned toward the kid. "Thanks. I have to go."

"Ah...no problem," he said. "I-I-I'm Eli. Eli Fleming. From math class?"

Oh, I knew him? Slowly it came to me. The kid who sat two rows over and seldom talked to anybody. Wait. I'd never heard him talk at all. And now I knew why. He stuttered. Yeah, kids would have a real tease-fest if they found out. "I'm Lauren Werthman. I'm new this year."

"I, um...know." The gap-toothed smile returned.

Alarm bells sounded in my head, which was ridiculous. So what if he knew my name? The teacher took attendance every day and called out everybody's name. Suddenly, though, staring at his ratty clothes and dirty hair, I had the urge to go home and take a shower.

He laid his pencil on the table and closed the sketchpad. "W-W-Was somebody trying to beat you up?"

How'd he know? "No, I...just didn't want to run into this girl."

He nodded. "I know what you mean."

I'll bet. I should have felt sorry for the guy, but I didn't. I just wanted to get away from him. He was creepy-looking. *You're scared of a pimple-faced, skinny dude who stutters? Stupid, Lauren. Really stupid.*

He pushed away from the table and stood, grabbing his sketchpad. "I-I-I can walk you out."

This was all I needed, to be seen with Stutter Boy. Like I wasn't already a target. *Be nice.* "No, thanks. My dad's outside waiting for me." *Please be there, Dad.*

Eli crossed the room with a strange glide-bounce step, and stopped next to me, frowning. "If your dad was outside, th-th-then why'd you come in here?"

OK. I had to act confident, be assertive, so I could get out of there. "I was trying to avoid somebody."

"Tiffany?"

"How'd you know?"

"I was, um, in the hall when you ran into her. She's a b—"

"Yeah, I have to go."

His face flushed red. "Um…w-w-well, it was nice talking to you, Lauren. Most people don't even notice me."

I hadn't. I didn't realize he was in my class. Would it have killed me to be nicer to the guy? He probably had zero friends and just wanted somebody to listen to him. "I'm sorry. It was a bad day, you know?"

"Yeah." He fumbled with his sketchpad, his pale arm too close to me.

I tried to squeeze past him, but he blocked the doorway. His sketchpad slipped from his hands and fell. Pages splayed open against the pebble-finished linoleum. He stooped, raking the pad toward him, and I bent over to hand it to him. My fingers reached it first, and right before I closed it, I noticed the pencil drawing on the first page. A girl. The likeness was unmistakable. Me. Handing him his sketchpad, my pulse throbbing against my neck, I scooted into the hallway.

My right shoe rubbed against my heel, adding another layer to the blister that had formed earlier. I should have worn socks, but it was too hot a day. I walked to the exit and pushed the door open.

Squinting when the late afternoon sun hit my face, I spotted Dad's truck sagging against the curb in front of the building, and I hurried over to it, yanked the handle, and slid into the passenger seat.

"Hey, kiddo. Sorry I'm late. The university called right when I was about to leave, and I had to take the call. You OK?"

"Yeah." The first sentence out of my mother's mouth would not have been, "Are you OK?" It would have been something like, "Have you lost your mind?" She would not say this to me in a calm voice. Her hands would gesture wildly while she ranted. But for right now, I was grateful Dad was the one who came to pick me up.

He started the truck and eased into traffic. A few blocks later, he braked for a red light and swiveled around to face me. "Pretty bad, huh?"

"Beyond belief."

"You want to talk about it?"

"Not really."

"Your principal called. We need to discuss what happened when we get home."

"I know."

Dad cranked up the oldies channel on the radio, and we listened to a rock song while he sang along, off-key, which made me laugh. "I'd have made a great back-up singer." He grinned.

"Uh-huh."

He played percussion on the steering wheel when a dance tune blasted through the speakers. This was the way it went for the rest of the trip home. We didn't talk, but Dad belted out the words to every song that played over the airwaves.

When we reached the house, all the windows were

dark except for a ghost-white light flickering across the walls in the living room, so I figured Mom was in there watching TV.

Dad hit the light switch, and as soon as he saw her, slumped in the recliner, asleep, the liveliness drained from his face. A *New York Times* best seller lay open in her lap, and her reading glasses had slid to the end of her narrow nose. On the lamp table beside her chair there was a stemmed glass, empty except for the quarter-sized pool of reddish liquid on the bottom.

She'd been drinking red wine. Lots of it. Morning, afternoon and early evening. If Dad said anything about it, she got all defensive and told me to tell him wine relaxed her. Yeah, she looked pretty relaxed. More like passed out. I guess staying awake was too painful.

Then we both noticed the wall.

Mom had been busy. My sister smiled down at us from at least a dozen family photographs. It was hard to believe Haley would never again come bursting through the door, bubbling with excitement, talking about her day in kindergarten.

Do not cry. Do not cry. Do not cry. It won't help.

Dad reached over, carefully lifted Mom's glasses from her face and set them on the side table. Massaging the bridge of his nose, he closed his eyes and said, "I can't deal with this now. We'll talk about it later." He pulled the afghan from the back of the couch and gently draped it over Mom before walking out of the room.

He couldn't deal with me, or he couldn't deal with Mom?

I trudged to my room, pulled the rubber stopper from the bottom of the flocked bunny bank—the one my parents had given me on Easter when I was eight—and shook out a handful of M & M's. I did this again and again until the bank was empty and my stomach cramped. Tomorrow I'd refill the bank, because Mom hadn't found this hiding place yet.

Stopping by the kitchen, I grabbed a diet soda to wash down the chocolate, trudged to the family room and booted up the computer. After doing an internet search on Rosa Parks, I printed information from several sites, and then I opened Word and started typing the essay for Mr. Hazzard.

"What are you doing?" Mom's words were slurred.

I hadn't heard her come in. Her hair, usually perfect, frizzed on either side of her face. She hadn't bothered to put on make-up, or crying had washed it away, because her eyes looked swollen and puffy. She leaned against the doorjamb, and I was sure if she hadn't done that, she would have fallen.

"Writing a report on Rosa Parks."

"For history class?"

"Uh-huh." Mr. Hazzard did teach history, and the report was for him, so it wasn't really a lie.

"We need to talk." She tucked some strands of hair behind one ear.

No, we didn't. Because Mom and I never talked, and when she drank too much, the talking escalated into yelling really fast. So I tried a diversion tactic. "Where's Dad?"

"He left. Didn't say where he was going. Did you meet with the school psychologist today?"

He deserted me? How could he leave me alone with Mom? I nodded. Meeting with Candra was the only decent thing about the whole day.

"And you're going to keep seeing her, right?"

"Yeah, I guess."

"You guess?" Her eyes widened. "You will keep seeing her, and if this doesn't help you, I will find another therapist and schedule you an appointment." She gestured in the air, punctuating every word, and her voice rose with each syllable. "I can't do this, Lauren. Do you understand what I'm saying? You have to adjust to your new school. I can't deal with phone calls from the principal about you."

Why didn't she say it? She couldn't deal with me. Well, I couldn't deal with her checking out of life, trying to act as if I wasn't there. She wanted me to stop causing problems so she wouldn't have to notice me. She'd rather pretend I didn't exist, because every time she looked at me, it reminded her of why Haley was no longer with us.

When she was done with the lecture, she mumbled, "I'm tired. I'm going to bed. But we will talk tomorrow."

I re-read the first sentence of my report: "In 1955 in Montgomery Alabama, Rosa Parks, an African-American woman, refused to give up her seat on the bus to a white person." Way to go, Rosa.

By the time I finished venting about why segregation was wrong, I'd written a thousand words. Exhausted, I headed for my room and reached under my mattress, feeling for the spiral notebook Miss Gladden had given me. When I found it, I sat on my bed, pillows propped behind my back and wrote:

"August 30th: Scary kids, scary teacher in detention. I don't want another one. Found Mom passed out in her chair. Does she have a drinking problem? If she does, it's probably my fault too. I've ruined her life. No wonder she hates me."

Afraid to close my eyes, afraid I'd dream about Haley, I lay in the dark, awake. Every time car lights flashed outside my window, I thought it was Dad coming home, but his truck didn't rumble into the driveway until twelve-thirty. By then, Mom had been asleep for hours.

Dad didn't nudge my door open. Instead, he turned the light on in the guest bedroom across from my room and closed the door behind him. An hour later, light still shone under his door.

When I couldn't keep my eyes open any longer, my mind drifted, having those crazy thoughts you get when you knew you were going to sleep. I was back at our old house, walking across the living room to check on Haley—her bedroom was on the other side—but when I peered in, she wasn't there. A small tee-shirt, a pair of shorts, and some cartoon character underwear lay in a crumpled heap beside her bed, and I ran, panicked, because I knew where she'd gone. "Haley, wait!" I screamed. "Haley!"

And then Dad was sitting beside me, stroking my hair. "It's OK, honey. It's only a dream."

No, it was real, and I kept reliving it, over and over.

11

First thing the next morning, I found Mr. Hazzard's history classroom. He sat hunched over his desk, reading, and when I hesitated near the doorway, he eyed me over the top of his glasses and motioned with pudgy fingers for me to come forward. "Miss Werthman," he said, taking a sip from an insulated coffee cup. "Bet you're glad you got to see me again."

Um, no.

He slurped another mouthful of coffee from the mug that had some convenience store logo on it. I wondered why he'd become a teacher. It was obvious he didn't like kids.

Sunlight slanted through the windows along one wall, and flecks of dust swirled in the air. Posters of early presidents hung above the whiteboard in the front of the room. An American flag attached to a pole stood anchored inside a stand on the right. To the left was a long table, and sitting on top was a box with what looked like mail slots stuffed with papers.

Mr. Hazzard's mouth curled up into a wicked-looking smile. "Good thing the school offers free coffee to teachers since you're not carrying a coffee shop cup. You have something else for me?"

Handing him the report, I stood next to his desk, not sure if I could leave.

"Rosa Parks, huh?" His eyes bored through mine.

I wanted to bolt out of there, but I swallowed and

forced myself to breathe.

"This'll do. OK, scram."

Right when I reached the doorway, he said in a taunting voice, "Oh, Miss Werthman?"

Now what? I turned.

He leaned back in his chair, hands clasped behind his head, smiling the same wicked smile. "Have a nice day."

By lunchtime, when I hadn't received any cryptic messages from Mr. Hazzard, I figured the report must have been acceptable. Going into the cafeteria was still awkward because the whole school knew I'd had an irregular mental health moment, but Jazz and Jonah had the same lunch period, so I tried to wait long enough so they'd get there before me. I'd forgiven Jonah for his "phobia" comment. I mean, what else could I do? Most everyone in school thought I was weird except for him, Jazz, and Candra. I couldn't afford to lose one of three friends.

The cafeteria was a beehive of activity. Chairs scraped against the linoleum floor. Voices droned together, creating a loud, continuous sound, almost like static on a radio. Silverware clinked against serving trays. Surveying the crowded, noisy room, I searched for Jonah and Jazz and finally spotted them at a table over by the sandwich line.

We pushed our trays along the steel counter, and Jonah turned up his nose at whatever unidentifiable entrée the cafeteria lady heaped onto his plate. It looked like lumps of leftover veggies and stringy meat smothered with white sauce.

We went back to the table they'd staked out and sat. I took a bite of the white sauce. It tasted like paste—I knew this because I could still remember sampling the kind they gave you in kindergarten—and let's just say they needed to disguise the vegetables because they were the really disgusting ones like lima beans and peas and cauliflower.

Jazz pushed her gelatin surprise around on the plate with her fork.

Surprise, it's inedible.

Jonah clasped his hands together and bowed his head for a few seconds. As usual, kids at nearby tables stared, but I didn't care. Jonah was my friend, and I'd gotten used to his weirdness, even if I didn't understand it.

"Soccer tryouts are a week from today," Jazz said casually as if she were repeating the weather forecast she'd heard on the morning news.

"You're going?" Jonah asked her, equally casually, like they'd rehearsed the whole speech. He chugged a mouthful of chocolate milk.

"Yes. Lauren?" Jazz's expression registered a look: Oh, here's a thought… "Why don't you come to soccer conditioning tomorrow? Then you can go with me to try-outs."

Had Candra put them up to this? Otherwise, Jazz had planned this whole scheme and talked Jonah into participating. Hadn't she noticed the inner tube of fat layered around my middle? You had to run to play soccer. Fast. My running days were history. "You want me to watch you try out?"

Jazz piled her plastic silverware, future landfill food, onto her plate. "Wouldn't it be fun if we both made the team? We could go to games together."

Waddling up and down a huge field, gasping for breath, trying not to get kicked or tripped by the opposing team while everybody laughed at my complete lack of physical endurance? Not my idea of fun. "Ah, let me think about it. No!"

"Come on," Jonah said. "You told us you used to play soccer. You have to find something you're good at. Use the gifts you were given."

I held up both hands to ward off the "God Given Gifts" speech, which he'd already shared with me several times.

"I'll pray for you, then," Jonah said, embarrassingly loud.

At least a dozen kids swiveled toward him.

Great, Jonah. Way to help maintain our weirdness status. "Please don't bother." I grabbed my tray, scraped my chair back, and stomped to the dirty tray window. A hair-netted woman with a mole on her chin waited on the other side to receive everybody else's garbage. I'd probably be her one day. This was a future I deserved.

Jonah and Jazz were still sitting at the table when I returned.

"I didn't mean to make you mad," Jonah said. "Sorry."

I had this terrible urge to feel his arms around me, to bury my head in his shoulder, to feel accepted by somebody who believed in a Higher Power, one I couldn't know because of what I'd done. Neither of my friends knew the specific reason I was seeing Miss Gladden, and they hadn't asked, but if they did know, they'd probably want nothing more to do with me. My sister died because of me. Even Jonah couldn't forgive me for that.

"It's OK," I said. "I shouldn't have snapped at you."

"About soccer conditioning," Jazz said, "maybe

you could just come and watch?"

"Sure."

"What are you doing later?" Jazz asked.

What I did every day after school. I'd go home, stuff my face with something, preferably chocolate in massive quantities, and then I'd take a nap. I didn't dream as much when it was still light outside. Nighttime was the worst, when I'd fall into a deep sleep, and the nightmares became too real. "Nothing. Why?"

"I thought maybe you would like to come to my house. We could play video games or watch a movie. Whatever you want to do."

"Hey," Jonah said, "can I come?"

"No!" We both said in unison.

"Just kidding," he said. "I have Youth Group at my church tonight, and I have to do chores before I go."

"So, you will come?" Jazz asked me.

"If it's OK with my mother." Like it wouldn't be OK. Mom would probably rubber stamp me moving in with Jazz.

"Good." Jazz smiled.

12

Jazz's house looked normal on the outside—white siding, gray shingled roof, charcoal-colored shutters framing the windows, but when I rang the bell and a woman answered the door, that was where "normal" ended.

There was a small red dot in the middle of her forehead. The wind caught her ankle-length gold dress, and the hemline fluttered around her sandals. Beads and sequins on her dress sparkled in the sunlight.

"Hello," she said, extending her hand. "You must be Lauren. I am the mother of Kavya. It is good to meet you." She shook my hand, and smiled a genuine smile, one as warm and bright as a birthday cake after the candles are lit, like the smile my mom used to give me before Haley died. "Please come in. Kavya is in her room."

I followed Mrs. Krishnan through their living room, across the Persian rug, past a giant tapestry labeled "Village Life" hanging on the wall. Three turquoise-colored throw pillows with elephant motifs lined the back of the burgundy sofa.

Mrs. Krishnan knocked on a door at the end of the hallway. "Kavya, Lauren is here."

Jazz opened the door and grinned at me. "Hi." Her mother left, and we flopped onto the paisley print spread that covered her bed. A carved wooden room divider stood next to her closet, like a mini dressing room. Inside their house, it was a whole different world.

"Why doesn't your mother call you Jazz?" I asked.

"It is not my birth name."

"Her dress was pretty."

"It's called a sari, the traditional dress women wear in India. The red dot on her forehead is called a bindi. Married Hindu women wear them as a form of protection for themselves and their husbands."

"Do you ever wear a sari?"

"I did in India, when I was younger, but I am not required to wear them here, unless we are going to Temple."

I didn't know much about Hinduism, but I did know they believed in reincarnation and karma. How you behaved in this life had a direct impact on your future lives.

A marble chess set sat on top of the rosewood table in the corner. "Do you play chess?"

"With my father. And you?"

"Me too. I mean, I play chess with my dad. My mom doesn't know how to play."

"Kavya!" a child yelled.

"I am busy!" Jazz yelled back. "My little sister, Tanvi. She is such a pest. Do you have any sisters or brothers?"

My stomach did a somersault and I stared at my hands. What could I tell her? I had a sister, but she died?

Jazz touched my arm. "I am sorry. Did I say something to upset you?"

Suddenly the door burst open and a little girl with huge brown eyes and a bow-shaped mouth stood in the doorway. "Mother said to tell you the ice cream is ready if you want some."

Jazz's sister looked about four or five. Haley was five when she died.

"She made kulfi," Jazz said. "Indian spiced ice cream. Would you like to try it?"

"Sure," I said in a shaky voice. Saved by the kulfi.

Jazz, Tanvi, and I ate our ice cream in the kitchen. Mrs. Krishnan was cooking dinner, and the room smelled of garlic, curry, and ginger.

"Can you stay and eat with us, Lauren?" Mrs. Krishnan asked.

Can I pack a suitcase and move in? "Thank you, but I have to get home." To what? A mother who hated me, and a dad who loved me, but whose marriage was falling apart? It was comfortable here. I wished I could stay forever.

After the ice cream, Jazz and I went back to her room and talked about the usual stuff: boys, teachers, homework assignments, and music we both liked. An hour later, I left and went home. Nobody was there, but I found a note tacked to the front of the refrigerator:

"Lauren:

Dinner is on the top shelf of the fridge. You can nuke it. Your father had a meeting tonight, and I went for a drive. See you soon. —Mom"

With the house to myself, I rummaged through the cupboards looking for something sweet, but who was I kidding? Mom didn't buy cookies or candy. I pulled out the foil-covered plate she'd left me, and I knew even before I lifted the covering what was underneath—something boring and low calorie—but I ate the skinless chicken breast, veggies, and grapes anyway. It was better than nothing. Afterward, I went to my room, refilled my bunny bank with miniature chocolates, and gorged myself with candy.

At ten-thirty neither one of my parents was home, so I wrote in the book Candra gave me:

"August 31

Where are Mom & Dad? Mom said she was taking a drive. I'm starting to get worried. Mom's been gone for hours. I hope she didn't drink before she left. I hate this house. I wish Dad would move out and take me with him.

What is it about Jonah? It's like I want to be with him all the time, which is weird because he's always saying stuff like, 'I'll pray for you,' which really bothers me. Jonah totally believes there is a God, but his God wouldn't care about someone like me."

Hours later, the sound of the garage door squealing open woke me. Car tires rolled into the garage and squeaky brakes ground to a halt. My mother was home. The door whined once again as she closed it.

I rolled out of bed and tiptoed out into the hallway, pushing the guest bedroom door open slightly. Covers pulled to his unshaven chin, Dad was snoring softly. Thank goodness they'd both come home.

13

Second period, when I approached Candra's doorway, she had her feet propped on her desk, her eyes were closed and she was leaning way back in her chair, ear bud inserted, singing worse than Dad, which I'd thought was impossible. It was hard to believe Mr. Bixby approved of her weird behavior, plus she didn't dress like the other staff members at Evington. Today she wore dark-washed jeans, hoop earrings the size of frozen juice lids, and a long-sleeved cotton tee-shirt with a metallic peace sign on the front.

I knocked on the door.

Her eyes flew open and she smiled. "Hey! How's my favorite journal writer?"

"Good." I had to work up the enthusiasm to say this, since it wasn't entirely true.

"Really?" She lowered her boot-clad feet to the floor and sat straight in her chair, eyes locking with mine. "Writing in your journal fixed all your problems and you don't need to talk to me today, huh?"

"Well, not that good." Of course, I needed to talk to her. The alternative was gym class, smelling chlorine and having a meltdown.

"OK. Come. Sit." She motioned with her hand.

Doggie bone, anyone?

Candra popped the pull tab on a can of diet cola. Was cola allowed? Her fingernails had a new coat of polish, deep purple, a totally anti-adult color. Silver bracelets jingled on both wrists. She took a long swallow. "Soda?"

"Thanks."

Fishing around in the small refrigerator, she scored another can and said, "Think fast." Without hesitation, she tossed the cola to me underhanded.

"Hey! Do you want it to explode all over me?"

"You have to be ready to deal with whatever life throws at you, my friend." She grinned.

Life didn't throw a can of diet pop at me. She did. Foam oozed out when I opened my drink, but I slurped it up before it could overflow onto the carpet.

"See, you can problem solve when something messy comes your way."

Foamy diet cola was not exactly like dealing with Tiffany, or Mom, or Haley's death.

"So." She cracked her knuckles, and then laced her fingers. "I thought we could talk about your parents today. What are they like?"

I shrugged, giving it some thought. I'd gotten pretty good at reading therapists over the last several months. If you saw enough of them, you learned how to play the game, give the right answers so they'd pronounce you cured, although I didn't mind meeting with Candra every day. She was the sort of person you couldn't stick a label on. Unique. Different than other doctors I'd known. I had to keep reminding myself she was the school psychologist.

"OK," she said, tapping a pencil against her desk. "Let's try this. Use one word to describe your mom and one word to describe your dad. Start with your mom."

Domineering. Depressed. Grumpy. Older than the constellations. Candra wouldn't like any of those adjectives. "I don't know."

"Sure you do. You're just afraid to say them. How about this, then. I'll say a word. If it describes your mom, I want you to nod. If it doesn't, shake your head. Got it?"

I got it, but I didn't like it. This was definitely a psych drill, a test to see what my relationship was like with my parents. I crossed my arms and pushed my back against my chair, disengaging, hoping she'd read my body language and stop the quiz.

Candra glanced up as if she were thinking and said, "Caring."

Fine. She wasn't reading my signals, so I'd have to concentrate on passing her stupid test. I nodded. Mom was a caring person. But not toward me. She used to be, but not anymore.

"How about, 'optimistic'?"

No way. Nothing made her happy. I shook my head.

"Let's switch to your dad now, OK? If I said, 'understanding' would that describe your dad?"

"Yes." Why were we talking about my parents? I thought this was about me and my problems.

"Good. How about 'judgmental'?"

"No." Never. Not even the day of the accident. He kept repeating things like, "It wasn't your fault. Don't blame yourself, honey. It was an accident."

"Let's return to your mother. Does 'judgmental' describe your mom?"

Although she never came right out and said it, Mom blamed me for Haley's death. I could tell by the way she looked at me. The tone of her voice. Everything had changed between us. Everything.

"Lauren? Does your mom often tell you what

you're doing wrong, or say your efforts aren't good enough?"

Not out loud, but yes. I saw it in her eyes. I shook my head slowly.

"You hesitated. Why?" Candra chose another pencil from the holder, a pencil with a weird, fuzzy creature where the eraser should have been, and she rolled it between her palms, causing the creature's hair to stand on end.

None of your business! Fail. Fail. I was failing this dumb test. "I thought I didn't have to talk about something if it made me uncomfortable."

"Correct. But you should know not talking about something speaks volumes to me."

"Great."

"How's school going? Are you fitting in?"

"I hang out with Jonah and Jazz, but other than them, I don't have any friends."

"You haven't been here very long, and you've identified with some good kids, so I think you're doing fine. People really only need a handful of friends. Some people only need one or two."

"I'm going with Jazz to soccer conditioning today after school."

Candra's eyes lit up. "Awesome! You're trying out for the team? I am so proud of you."

"Um, no. Jazz asked me to, but I don't think I'm ready to play sports." Truth: I was addicted to food, especially not-good-for-me food, and until I could stop stuffing my face, which might never happen, I wouldn't be ready to play sports.

"Oh, well, it's good you're going with her. It's important to support friends."

"How many friends do you have?" Time to

employ the let's-talk-about-you tactic. If you could get the therapist to start talking about themselves, you'd throw them off track, and they'd forget about questioning you, at least temporarily.

She leaned back in her chair and cracked her knuckles. "Depends on your definition of a friend. I consider most people I know my friends, but I only have a couple really close friends, and by close friends, I mean people I confide in. People I trust with my deepest secrets and toughest problems."

I didn't trust anyone that much. Well, maybe Dad. But I had no desire to tell Jazz or Jonah about Haley, because what would they think of me then?

"Do you trust me, Lauren?"

"I guess. Maybe." I was afraid to be totally honest with her, because I didn't want her to stop liking me.

She smiled. "Didn't realize I'd asked a multiple choice question. Which is it?"

"Not entirely?"

"Good enough. I'll accept your answer."

"Do I ever have to go to gym class?" I knew at some point, I would. Gym was required.

"Yes, but not anytime soon. What happened that day in the hall? Can you tell me?"

We were talking like friends, not like therapist/patient. She didn't give me the Oh-you-poor-kid look. I wanted to tell her about Haley, I really did, but I was afraid she'd treat me differently, like Mom did. I shook my head.

She held up her hands. "It's fine. You'll tell me one day. Principal Bixby knows your story, but I won't ask him, Lauren. I want it to come from you. When you trust me enough to tell me the truth, then I've done my job well."

The bell rang. I thanked her for the soda and charged out of her office. I was stressed, and I needed chocolate. The only private place was the restroom, so I headed for the nearest one, pushed the door open and breezed through it. Walking to the farthest stall, I shut myself inside and unwrapped mini Hershey bars in fast forward speed. I waited for the payoff, the better mood that always arrived after I binged on something sweet, and I didn't have to wait long, just a few seconds. The problem was, the good mood disappeared fast, and then I felt stupid and fat. Once again, I'd given into temptation. I didn't have control over food, it had control over me.

14

Girls dressed in tee-shirts, shorts, and athletic shoes sprinted effortlessly onto the field and lined up, waiting their turn to kick a soccer ball at the net. If I hadn't promised Jazz I'd come, I would have left because Tiffany was there too. Her long legs were a golden tan from the summer sun, and her sleek ponytail bobbed as she bounced gracefully on the toes of her name-brand shoes. Cheerleader worshipers, all of them male, whistled from the sidelines.

Soccer conditioning started in five minutes. Jazz should have been there by then, but she wasn't. I was feeling very self-conscious in my shorts—ones that fit me two months ago, but now seemed determined to inch up my inner thighs with every step I took. Whenever I reached for the shorts to pull the fabric back down, I was certain everybody was staring at me and laughing.

Walking across the field seemed like the longest walk of my life, but I finally sidled up to the bleachers and dropped onto the lowest seat.

"Lauren!"

I knew the voice—Eli Fleming, but it was too late to run. Did he follow me? I turned, and there he was, giant stepping his way from the highest bleacher, his gap-toothed smile wide, the sketchpad he always carried tucked under his arm like an extra appendage. *Please tell me there are no more sketches of me.*

I smiled back—early childhood training courtesy of Mom and Dad—even though I wanted to disappear.

"H-H-Hi, Lauren." Eli's gaze darted between me and the ground. "It's hot," he managed to say without tripping over his words. "I-I-I have water, if you, um, get…thirsty." He crouched in front of me, and there was ground-in dirt on the knees of his jeans, and the big toe on his right foot had pushed partway through his sneaker.

"No, thanks." If I was lost in the middle of nowhere on a hundred-degree day, I wouldn't accept a drink from this guy.

"It's no problem." He yanked on the zipper of his book bag and it separated a few inches but wouldn't budge. Narrowing his eyes, he wrestled with it. "S-S-Stupid bag!"

"It's OK, I'm fine."

"No, um, the water's right here." Eli pried the zipper apart. *Rrrrip.* The backpack lay on the ground, broken. He rose, victorious, holding a smudged bottle in front of his stained white tee-shirt.

"I'm not thirsty. Really."

I glanced past Eli. Tiffany was pointing me out to Courtney Abrahms, her BFF. Both of them grinned as if I were the punch line of a joke. Tiffany jogged over to me, a fake smile plastered on her face, with Courtney close behind her.

"Hey, Lauren!" Courtney said, as if we were old friends. "You're trying out for soccer? Seriously?"

Tiffany shot me a smirk and smiled her approval at Courtney.

"Why not?" I blurted out. Periodically my brain failed to communicate with my mouth.

Tiffany's eyes widened and her mouth hung open

before curving into a smile. "Well, this should be entertaining."

Way to go. Now I had no choice. I had to try out for the team. A year ago, I could have outrun Tiffany, could have sent balls flying past her, but now, hundreds of chocolate bars later, I could hardly manage a jog without breaking into a sweat.

Tiffany leaned toward me, one perfect knee bent, and pushed her hand against her hip. Her shiny blue shorts barely covered her rear end, and her v-neck tee-shirt took a nosedive to very noticeable cleavage. "Did Eli come to watch you?" she said. "I didn't know you two were going out."

Eli's face turned crimson. He shoved the water bottle into his backpack, now on the waiting list for a zipper transplant. "We're, um...just friends."

Really? Since when? Talking to him twice meant we were friends?

The gym teacher, Miss Torrens, (I knew her name because it was listed on my class schedule) ran to center field and blew the whistle attached to a cord around her neck.

"Let's go, girls!" She checked her watch. "We have exactly one hour and ten minutes before I'm outta here, so let's not waste time."

As if choreographed, everyone turned to watch Jazz streak onto the field. Her purse strap swung back and forth, a book bag banged against her side, and her trumpet case thumped her knees. Long strands of hair had escaped a ponytail holder, and she brushed them away from her face as she ran.

"Miss Krishnan," Miss Torrens said. "We were speaking of wasting time. My time. Which you are doing by showing up late for conditioning."

"I am sorry," Jazz said. "Band rehearsal ran late."

Miss Torrens held up her hand. "Your problem, not mine. Everybody form a line facing the goal." She clapped her hands. "Hustle!"

In under ten seconds, about twenty girls fell into line. Miss Torrens pulled a clipboard from a duffle bag on the ground. She freed the pencil nested in short cropped hair behind her ear. "When it is your turn, state your name, grade, and how many years you've played organized soccer. Then the goalie will roll the ball to you, and I want you to take a shot at the net. If you are the goalie, try to block the shot. Everybody clear?"

Heads bobbed in unison. Name, rank and serial number. Was she related to Mr. Hazzard?

Jazz and I were sandwiched in the middle of the line. She touched my shoulder. "What are you doing? I thought you were watching?"

Before I could answer, Miss Torrens pointed. At me. "Werthman, play goalie."

What? How did she know who I was? Mr. Bixby must have pointed out the girl who got a get-out-of-gym-free card. Just what I needed, everybody staring at me—the klutzy, overweight girl—who also happened to be a head case.

Eli, the kid who previously never spoke in public, clapped enthusiastically. "Go, Lauren!"

OK, maybe there was a God, and he'd condemned me to live in high school hell.

"Yeah, go Lauren!" Tiffany clapped. Six or seven Tiffany wannabes joined in, and by the amused looks on their faces, they were enjoying my discomfort.

Shoulders slumped, I shuffled to the goal. Why did the teacher do this to me?

Miss Torrens rested her hands on her hips. "Sometime today, Werthman."

I turned and faced them. Miss Torrens hurled a ball at me and, unbelievably, I caught it.

The first girl, taller than a redwood, stepped forward. I was toast. She announced her stats: Emilee, tenth grade, and she played last year.

A whistle blew. Miss Torrens looked annoyed. "Let's go, Miss Werthman. Roll the ball to her."

I obeyed, and the girl advanced the ball from side to side until she was within twenty feet of the net.

Pay attention. Block the shot.

The ball made contact with the side of her foot and sailed high, full force, toward the right side of the net. With outstretched arms, I dove sideways and the impact knocked me to the ground, but I had the soccer ball clutched in my hands.

"Amazing!" Jazz yelled. "Nice stop."

"Not bad, Werthman," Miss Torrens said. "Next girl. Let's go."

A fluke. Had to be. I couldn't do it again. One elbow hurt and I'd banged up a knee. This was crazy. I wasn't goalie material. I limped into position again and rolled the ball to a short girl who looked like a middle school kid. She drew her foot back and made contact, but this shot stayed low, so I kicked it, and it flew to the middle of the field. Oh. My. Gosh. I could not believe it went so far.

I continued to surprise myself by stopping all but two balls from burrowing into the goal. When half the girls had taken shots, and it was Jazz's turn, Miss Torrens pointed at Courtney. "You. Abrahms. Play goalie. Werthman, get back in line."

"I hate playing goalie," Courtney whined as she

sauntered to the net.

"What was that, Abrahms?" Miss Torrens said, giving her the classic teacher frown: wrinkled forehead, tight, straight-line lips.

"Nothing," she said. She did an eye roll, but Miss Torrens didn't notice.

Courtney pivoted in front of the goal, bowled the soccer ball toward Jazz, and she smacked it.

You know the game kids play where they try to tag people who run past them, but the taggers aren't allowed to move their feet? That was what Courtney looked like when she went after the ball. Pathetic.

"Abrahms!" Miss Torrens said. "You have to move when you're goalie. Like Werthman did. You can't just stand there afraid to go after the ball because you might chip a nail!"

From then on, Miss Torrens became my favorite teacher, even though I hadn't officially had her as a teacher yet.

I grinned at Jazz when she raced past me on her way to the back of the line.

My turn. Courtney hated me because Tiffany hated me. Was it possible to pitch a curve ball with a soccer ball? Courtney wanted me to look bad, and she'd do everything possible to make it happen. She heaved the ball at me and I ran to meet it, well more like scuttled, and it careened off the side of my foot, sailed high into the air and landed way left of the net, totally missing. Courtney laughed. Next time I'd score, even if this wasn't a game.

Jazz gave me a high-five. "Nice try. You'll bury the next one."

Bury. The funeral. My little sister, not breathing, lying inside a polished, wooden box. Haley was afraid of the dark, and it would turn dark inside there. For one irrational moment, when the funeral director closed the lid, I'd wanted to lift it and let the sunshine flood that dark space. Then the funeral director gestured toward a row of chairs facing the casket, expecting me and Mom and Dad to sit there, forcing us to stare at it.

I bent over, hands on my knees, feeling dizzy, my heart thumping way too fast.

"Lauren?" Somebody called my name. Jazz shook my arm. "Hey, what's wrong? It's your turn."

"Y-Y-You can do it, Lauren." Eli the Stalker gave me a thumbs up.

I wanted Jonah there cheering for me, not Eli. But he'd gone to a youth group meeting at his church. If I told him I was trying out for the team would he come?

Focus.

Courtney hurled the ball at me.

Connect this time. Don't miss. I ran, felt the fat jiggle on my legs. The kick soared high and...*oh no!* The black and white bomb smacked Courtney in the face and she screamed, staggered backward, and fell to the ground like a deer that'd been shot.

I stood paralyzed until Miss Torrens yelled, "Werthman, run inside and get an icepack from the nurse." In seconds, everybody rushed over to Courtney who lay writhing on the ground, her hands covering her face.

"It hurts!" Courtney shrieked.

"Move, Werthman!" Miss Torrens said.

Bursting across the field toward the school, I nearly plowed into Eli. "I'll go with you," he said.

"I don't need your help!"

Less than five minutes later, out of breath and

sweaty, I raced to the mob surrounding my victim and pushed my way through to Miss Torrens.

Courtney was sobbing, close to hysterical. Blood oozed from her lip.

"She did it on purpose," Tiffany said. "She aimed right at her!"

Miss Torrens pressed the ice pack against Courtney's mouth. "She wasn't supposed to stop the ball with her face."

Because I smiled—how sick was that?—I had to cover my mouth with my hand.

Courtney reached for the bag, but Miss Torrens grabbed her hand. "Keep the ice on. It'll help with the swelling."

Courtney's eyes bulged. "Swelling?" she blubbered.

"We'll call your parents." Miss Torrens helped Courtney to her feet. "That's it for today, girls. See you tomorrow."

Supported by Tiffany and Miss Torrens, Courtney hobbled toward the building.

Somebody touched my arm. I whipped around.

Eli stood there, grinning. "C-C-Couldn't have happened to a nicer person."

Another girl let out a low whistle. "I'm glad I'm not you, Werthman."

Why had I stayed for soccer conditioning? Ever since the accident, my life was just one disaster after another, and even when something good happened to me, it didn't last.

15

I made it through first period the next day. Relief flooded through me as I headed for Candra's office, a place I'd learned to recognize as a safety zone.

Through the doorway, I saw Harley, a marathon runner on his hamster treadmill, but there was no sign of Candra. Ditching my book bag on the floor, I opened the mini fridge, grabbed a diet pop, and slouched into a chair. "Help yourself to a soda anytime," Candra had told me. "You don't need to ask."

The treadmill stopped squeaking, and Harley stared at me, nose twitching, whiskers trembling.

"What? She gave me permission."

His beady eyes remained focused on mine. He sat up like a puppy doing tricks and sniffed the air.

"I'm not lying. She did."

"You and the hamster having a nice chat?" Tiffany's perfectly proportioned body filled the doorway. "Maimed anybody today, Werthman?"

"It was an accident." The stench of her perfume or body lotion or whatever the citrus smell was, assaulted my nose and caused my throat to constrict. She flicked back her color-from-a-box blonde hair.

"Uh-huh. Pretty convenient though, because you don't like Courtney, do you?"

"Who does?" Spontaneous stupidity. It was a gift. One I wished I didn't have.

"Cute, Werthman. You don't sound very sorry for

what you did."

"Maybe you should look up 'accident' in the dictionary. That is if you know how to use a dictionary." What is it that makes you say dumb things when you're verbally attacked? It usually makes everything a whole lot worse.

"You're the expert on accidents. You seem to be around when they happen, right?"

She was right. I was a jinx. People got hurt or died when I was around. A current of heat traveled from the small of my back all the way up to my face.

"Oops. Sorry. You look upset. Maybe your meds aren't working. I'm sure Miss Gladden can refer you to a good shrink so you can have that checked out before they lock you away somewhere."

Nothing would have felt better than to punch her in the mouth and give her a fat lip, but I'd promised myself no more detentions. "Don't you have anything better to do? Like go to your next class?"

She held up a slip of paper. "Hall pass. I'm using the restroom as we speak."

"Yeah, you have an interesting way of 'using' it."

"Shut up, Lard Butt." She flashed a mouthful of perfect teeth. Her parents must have paid a fortune to the orthodontist. "So you transferred here from a school in Minnesota, right?" She checked her nails. Her mouth quivered before she ran a new coat of lip gloss over it. "Did you know this school uses student aides in the office?"

"Fascinating. What other useless trivia do you know?"

"The student files are in locked cabinets, but if you know the right person…"

"What are you trying to say, Tiffany?"

She flicked her hair, checked her hideously long nails again and shrugged. "Oh, nothing. Just that you can find out all kinds of interesting things about other kids if you browse through those files." She looked me straight in the eyes. "Take for instance, your file. I mean, they could probably make a movie out of the stuff in your file."

Oh, God. Breathe. She's bluffing. She doesn't know about Haley. But what if she did? What if she was telling the truth? It took all my concentration to keep my voice even. "You'd get suspended for snooping in confidential files."

"Me? No, I never read your file. But the thing is, Werthman, somebody did. And kids are talking about you."

Yeah, maybe, but they were talking about me kicking a ball into Courtney's face, not about my old life in Minnesota. She hadn't said one thing to prove she knew what had happened to my sister. "Why don't you stop playing games, huh? You're not very good at it."

Her smile slipped into a scowl for a couple of seconds before she retrieved it. "Seriously, you need to have them reevaluate your meds. I mean, your attitude stinks. You're such a mouthy witch."

"Something I can do for you, Tiffany?" Candra stepped around Tiffany, two cloth grocery bags in hand. She set the bags on her desk and removed her black, leather jacket. The trio of silver bracelets on her arms jangled.

"No, um, I was just leaving." Tiffany stalked through the doorway.

"Sit," Candra said to me. "I heard about Courtney. It was unfortunate you were the one who kicked the ball." She flung the leather jacket over a chair back and stocked the fridge with the pop.

"Yeah, tell me about it."

"Tiffany came to give you a hard time, right?"

I nodded. "Why do bad things keep happening to me?"

"Bad things happen to everybody, sweetheart." She snatched a diet pop and pulled the tab, sitting cross-legged in the chair opposite me. "How'd soccer conditioning go otherwise? You think you'll be ready for tryouts?"

"I'm not trying out now. How can I?"

"You mean because you hurt somebody?"

"Yeah." Jonah talked about gifts. Well this was my gift. Hurting people.

"Did you intentionally aim the ball at her?"

Heat flushed my face. "No! It just happened."

"So you're saying it was an accident? It wasn't your fault?"

"Yeah, that's what I'm saying."

She scribbled some notes on a tablet. I assumed it was about my messed up state of mind.

"Do you like playing soccer?" She took a drink of pop.

"I used to." When I could actually play.

"Then if you keep going to conditioning, and if you make the cut, why can't you play on the team?"

"Because they don't want me there."

"Who are 'they'?"

"Tiffany. Courtney. All of them."

"Jazz wants you there."

"Most of them hate me. And besides, I can't keep up. A soccer field is huge. There's a lot of running."

"Funny, I didn't think you were a wimp."

My pulse galloped against my neck. I stood, shoved my chair back, and stormed to the door.

"Stop. Come back."

"Why?" I whirled around, a familiar lump in my throat, the one that meant I was about to cry, and I sure didn't want it to happen there in her office.

"Lauren, you are a strong, capable, young woman with above average intelligence."

Oh. Did she mean it? I shuffled to the chair opposite Candra's and slouched into it, staring at the shag rug. "Tiffany said one of her friends read my student file, but they couldn't have, right?"

"I don't see how."

"Would the stuff about my sister be in there?"

"Mr. Bixby talked to your parents, so yes, it was probably recorded in your file."

"This will never go away. Why am I even trying?"

"Look at me."

I met her gaze, and one thing was clear: Candra wasn't coming to my pity party.

"Was what happened to your sister your fault, Lauren?"

"Yes...no. I don't know, OK? I was supposed to watch Haley, and I didn't, so yeah, it was my fault."

Candra rose and shut the door. "So your negligence caused her to get hurt?"

I lowered my voice to a whisper. "Yes."

"Did you plan to hurt your sister? Did you know it was going to happen?"

"No!"

"Sounds like it wasn't your fault then. Like kicking the soccer ball into Courtney's face wasn't your fault."

"It's not the same. I was babysitting Haley, and I didn't pay attention to her."

"So you made a mistake. Everybody makes mistakes, Lauren. You have to forgive yourself."

"This was more than a mistake, OK?" I let Haley die.

"OK. Sorry. I can see this is upsetting you."

"Can I go now, please?" I wanted to curl up in bed, under the covers and hibernate in my room forever.

"Sure. Lauren? Don't give other people the power to stop you from living your life."

What if I didn't deserve a life? I nodded to show her I understood so she'd let me leave.

"At least think about trying out for soccer. It would be good for you." Candra patted my arm and then slipped back inside her office. She inserted an ear bud, sank into her chair and propped boot-clad feet on the desk.

16

At eleven-thirty that night, I sat cross-legged on my bed and grabbed the journal Candra had given me. I clicked the ball-point pen in my hand and wrote: "I must be crazy, because tomorrow I'm going back to soccer conditioning. Not because Candra said I should, but because she was right. I shouldn't let Tiffany and Courtney stop me from doing things. Why do I keep getting myself into awkward situations? Truth: because I can't stand people who act like they're better than me. Like Tiffany and Courtney. Tiffany has a big mouth and she's pushy, and I hate pushy people."

The house was quiet except for a tree branch outside my window tapping its bony fingers against the glass. The only light on besides mine shone under the door of Dad's newly claimed office down the hall. Before Mom went to bed, a little after nine, she'd hardly spoken to either of us. Of course, she still wasn't speaking to Dad directly. Everything went through me… "Tell your father the mail's on the counter. Ask your father to please pass the pepper." I was so sick of it. Why did they even bother to stay together?

Maybe I'd talk to Dad and see how he felt. He had to be tired of this too. We could both leave and find a new place. Mom would be happy to get rid of me.

These thoughts, when analyzed, terrified me. We couldn't leave Mom. She had a drinking problem. Dad knew it and so did I. Something bad might happen if we left her alone. And in spite of everything, I could tell he still loved her. He'd never agree to move out.

I closed the notebook and slid it between the mattresses way in the middle of the bed, so when Mom changed the sheets, she wouldn't find it. I didn't want anybody to read it, because I couldn't reveal everything in my heart, or I'd die of exposure. Some things were just too private.

Somebody knocked on my door. "Lauren?" Dad said. "Permission to enter the queen's chambers?"

I did an involuntary eye roll. "Really, Dad?"

The door squealed open and Dad stood there, leaning against the jamb, his hair wild like an overgrown lawn, his striped pajama bottoms wrinkled, and his white tee-shirt coffee-stained. "You have plans after school tomorrow?"

"Yeah. I plan to humiliate myself on the soccer field. I'm going to soccer conditioning, so I can try out for the team."

He beamed. "Really? That's terrific, honey! I should be able to get away from work if you need a ride home."

"Thanks. Why did you ask if I had plans?"

"Oh, it's not important. We can talk about it when you get home tomorrow." His eyes twinkled. He was up to something. Something he thought I'd like.

"OK."

Did Mom know about Dad's surprise? Doubtful. My happiness was not her top priority. Haley's happiness had mattered to Mom a whole lot more than mine.

Dad crossed the room, sat on the edge of my bed, and the mattress squeaked in protest. "When's the first game? I want to come."

"Dad! This is just conditioning. I still have to try out for the team."

"You'll make it. I know you will. If you want something bad enough, you go after it. And I love watching somebody I love play soccer."

Mom used to insist we arrive thirty minutes early for Haley's games so she could get a front row seat on the bleachers. She never missed a game. Dad missed a few, because of work, but he came most of the time. If Mom came to my games now, it would remind her of Haley. "Could you not mention this to Mom?"

"Of course not! She's your mother, Lauren. She wants to be involved in your life."

No she doesn't. "But it'll upset her if she finds out about soccer, because it'll remind her of Haley."

Dad lifted my chin. "It might be hard for her, but she'll work through it. Your mom's a strong lady."

Disappointment crossed Mom's face whenever she looked at me, as if she were disappointed I was still alive, and Haley, her darling little girl, was not. She and Dad were still sleeping in separate rooms. Did he call that working through things?

He ruffled my hair. "Well, we'd better get some sleep. I'm proud of you, Lauren! Being part of the soccer team will be a good thing for you, you'll see. It's always easier to fit in when you're part of a team."

"Maybe. Goodnight, Dad. Love you."

He smiled and crow's feet magically appeared at the corners of his eyes. "Love you more."

I was awake for an hour and finally decided to go downstairs to get something to eat—my fast-fix solution for all of life's problems. Whatever emotion I didn't feel like dealing with, I'd squelch it with food. Yeah, I knew what I was doing, and I knew it was only a temporary solution, but I'd feel better, at least for a few minutes, which beat never feeling good.

Barefoot, I padded down the stairs, plush carpeting soft under my feet, patches of moonlight casting a faint glow, lighting my way. I didn't want to turn on the light and risk somebody seeing me.

When I reached the kitchen, I crossed the room, flicked on the light above the sink, and debated with myself about what I wanted to eat. Tortilla chips dipped in ranch dressing? Soda crackers dragged through butter? Chocolate?

I'd run out of chocolate bars. I hadn't had a chance to get to a store yet. Mom had a chocolate stash she didn't think anybody knew about, but I'd found it last week behind the canned vegetables. I just took a few miniature peanut butter cups, because I didn't want her to know somebody had been into them. The only way she could really tell was if she counted them every day, and I couldn't see even Mom sinking so low.

When I opened the cupboard and pushed the cans aside, I didn't find the candy. She must have suspected Dad or I had discovered her stash and moved it. I opened the cereal cupboard, searching for chocolate. Nothing. Maybe she got creative.

I stooped down and pulled out the front row of pots and pans in the lower cupboard, and that was when I saw it...a half-empty bottle of scotch. Behind it was another one. So she'd stopped drinking wine and moved on to hard liquor. Did Dad know?

I replaced the pans and was closing the cupboard when I heard Mom's voice and nearly jumped out of my skin.

"Looking for something?"

Turning to face her, I tried to keep my voice

sounding normal so she wouldn't know how shocked I was. "No, um, I couldn't sleep."

"So you thought you'd come down here and rearrange the pots and pans?" There were dark circles under her eyes. She wore baggy, wrinkled pajamas, and she looked thinner than she had before we'd moved here. She never ate much dinner. She'd stopped eating bread altogether, saying it was too fattening.

"No, I was going to make hot chocolate," I lied. "Why are you up?"

"I couldn't sleep either."

So you thought you'd come down here and drink scotch until you passed out? Nice, Mom. There was no difference between her and me. We were both trying to make ourselves feel better, her with booze, me with food.

Wasn't drinking alone one of the signs of an alcoholic? Dad probably thought she was asleep in the guest bedroom, exactly what she wanted him to believe.

She walked to the fridge, opened it, and pulled out the skim milk. She poured some milk into a cup and then popped it into the microwave. "Warm milk will help you sleep, but you don't need a snack. Every time I go to the mall to buy you clothes, I have to buy you a larger size."

Thanks. Like I hadn't noticed zipper teeth refusing to come together and buttons that wouldn't fasten.

The microwave beeped. She handed me the cup of milk. "How's school going? You're still seeing the school psychologist, right?"

"Fine and yes." Maybe I'd dump all the scotch down the drain, but it wouldn't do any good. She'd just buy more and hide it in a different spot. Still, if I did dump the bottles, what could she do about it? She couldn't confront me, because then she'd have to acknowledge she'd hidden them, and she'd be afraid I'd tell Dad.

"When does she think you'll be able to take gym class? You don't get enough exercise."

Look who's talking. She rarely left the house, and when she was home, she preferred to stay in her room with the door closed to shut out the world.

"I'm going to soccer conditioning tomorrow. It's every night after school for a week."

One of Mom's eyebrows arched, but she didn't look at me, she looked away, and I knew she was thinking about Haley. Even at five, Haley was athletic. Whatever sport she tried, she excelled at. "Well...that's good," Mom said. She swallowed like she had an avocado pit stuck in her throat, and then she left me standing in the kitchen, alone.

17

I didn't see Courtney in school the next day, but rumors swirled through the hallways and classrooms. Rumors like: Courtney had to have stitches. Her lip was swollen and black and blue. She looked like a relative of Frankenstein.

The situation wouldn't improve when Courtney returned to school either, because she'd become a walking billboard, advertising what I'd done to her. She'd say stuff like, "Look what that freak Werthman did to me."

Turning the corner, I veered into Candra's office, my safe haven, and heard...nothing. The hamster wheel wasn't squeaking. I bent down and peered into the cage, but Harley wasn't burrowed under the shredded wood chips in the bottom. He wasn't anywhere. Oh, God. Did he die? Was it because of me? Because Lauren Werthman, the jinx, came here every day?

The teacher's lounge door swung open and Candra emerged, carrying a tall wastebasket. As soon as I heard the scratching sounds, I let out the breath I hadn't realized I'd been holding.

"What's wrong? You look pale." She set the wastebasket down. Inside, Harley clawed at the sides, but slid back down as if the trashcan was made out of ice.

"I thought..."

"You thought something happened to Harley."

"Yeah."

"I cleaned his cage. He's fine, as you can see."

When I reached in to pet him, his whiskers tickled my fingers.

"Could you do me a favor?" Candra brushed past me, through her office door, and I followed her. Scooping up Harley with one hand, she raised the cage door and gently set him inside.

"Sure. What?"

"Well, I need somebody to take care of Harley for about a week. Feed him, fill his water dish, talk to him, that sort of thing. Oh, and if he's scared—you'll know because he'll start shaking—just sing a couple verses of 'Twinkle, Twinkle Little Star.' Calms him right down. He might need his cage cleaned once while I'm gone too."

A week? She couldn't leave me for a whole week. What if I needed her? What was I supposed to do second period? I swallowed the "No!" that tried to explode from my lips. "Why?" I finally mumbled.

"It's personal. I have to take some time off."

My palms grew sweaty. She didn't know who she was asking. She didn't know how irresponsible I was.

"I trust you, Lauren. I know you'll keep Harley safe."

Safe. I didn't keep my sister safe. Did this mean I had to go to gym class?

"His food's right here." She slid open a side desk drawer and removed a box with a picture of a hamster on the front. "You just fill the little dish...Lauren are you listening?"

My knees felt mushy, like they might not hold me up. When I looked at the overheard fluorescent lights, white spots danced in front of my eyes like a too bright camera flash.

Candra touched my shoulder. "Oh, sweetheart, I'm sorry. I was so preoccupied with my own plans, I didn't explain what this will mean for you. I have a confession. Ready?"

I nodded. The word "confession" momentarily stopped my own panicky thoughts.

"Here goes." She smiled. "I'm human. Who would have thought? The school psychologist is flawed and vulnerable like everybody else."

Vulnerable how? Was there a death in her family? Was Candra sick?

Harley's wheel squeaked as he ran at a furious pace.

"You're worried about second period, right?" Candra said, tossing me a can of pop.

I blew out a breath. Candra had problems of her own. I didn't know what they were, but she was admitting to me some heavy stuff was going on in her life too. Or maybe it was something good. Like she was getting married or going on a trip. "Yeah, there's that…and how am I gonna do this without you?"

"Do what? You only come here one period a day, and the rest of the time, you're on your own, handling…life. I've talked to Principal Bixby. He's agreed to let you work as a student aide next week during second period. Whatever awful thing happened before you moved here, well, I think once you get past it, you'll be an even stronger person than before."

How did you get past letting your little sister drown? I wanted to tell her what happened to Haley, and I even thought she'd understand and reassure me, but she had something else on her mind today.

"So…you want to talk about it?"

For a second, she looked surprised and then she laughed. "Who's the student and who's the counselor here?"

"Well even counselors need to vent sometimes, right?"

"You know what? I really like you, sweetheart. But don't worry about me. I'm fine. And I'll be back before you know it. Kiss?"

What? She reached inside her center desk drawer and retrieved a bag of chocolate candies, tossing me one and peeling the foil off another for herself. *Oh.*

"I'm addicted to chocolate," she said.

Yeah, me too. In two seconds, I'd chewed and swallowed the piece of candy. And I wanted more.

"Would you like another one?" she asked.

"Uh-huh." I could have eaten the whole bag. Now that I knew it was in her desk drawer, I wondered whether I'd be able to leave it alone when she was gone next week. Just to be safe, I'd bring my own candy from home in case I was tempted.

Candra threw me another chocolate and sank into a chair. "Let me ask you something, Lauren. If this was your bag of candy, how long would it last?"

I shrugged. Maybe a few hours. Maybe a whole day, depending on how it was going.

"I'm asking because you mentioned you'd put on some weight since your sister's accident. Here's the deal: when something's bothering us, sometimes we use food to make ourselves feel better."

How would she know? She'd never gorged herself with chocolate and then felt guilty about it later. Extra fat didn't jiggle from her arms, and her jeans didn't look as if the seams were ready to rip. She looked good, like a size eight good.

"Do you ever eat to feel better, Lauren?"

Yeah, on a regular basis. How did she see inside me? I nodded.

"You don't feel good about it, do you?"

"No." But it helped me make it through the day.

She rolled the top of the bag shut and stuffed it back into the drawer. "I have another confession to make." She folded her hands, sighed. "When I was your age, I was fat. I mean really fat, like obese, and I was addicted to food. I didn't eat to live, I lived to eat."

Her? No way. "But you're not fat now. How'd you stop overeating?"

"You using the journal I gave you?"

"Every day."

"Good. Because now in addition to jotting down your thoughts, every time you get the urge to eat too much, to binge eat, I want you to resist it, and make a note of how you feel instead. Scared. Bored. Lonely. Whatever the emotion is, jot it down. And you know what? Pretty soon, you'll see a pattern emerge, and often you can distract yourself or in the future, avoid the situation that made you feel bad. If you can wait awhile, like fifteen or twenty minutes, the craving will usually pass."

I didn't believe her, but I was willing to try. It must have worked for her.

"Look for good distractions. Like sports. And using your brain to problem solve. And helping other people. Don't replace one bad habit with another. For instance, don't take up smoking to stop yourself from overeating. Understand?"

"Yeah."

"You have my cell number. If at any time during

the next week you need to talk to me, just call. If I don't pick up, leave a message, and I'll get back to you as soon as I can. Or chat with me on Facebook. You're gonna be fine. Will you take care of Harley for me?"

"Sure."

She touched the tip of my nose. "Hang in there, sweetheart, OK? You deserve to be happy."

I walked to the doorway, turned, and said, "Good luck...on your trip."

"Thank you."

Merging with the stream of students out in the hallway, her words scrolled across my mind: "You deserve to be happy."

18

As I walked toward the soccer field, my shorts shimmied up my legs, and the skin on my inner thighs rubbed together. The late afternoon sun scorched the back of my neck. My shin guards, under the long socks, stuck to my sweaty legs. I dreaded this practice because of what had happened at the last one, and because of the heat.

I could feel everyone watching me. I thought about Rosa Parks—the black woman who'd boarded a bus meant for white people—and how uncomfortable she must have been. Nobody wanted her there. She didn't belong.

Tiffany stood at the edge of the field, chatting with two boys who seemed mesmerized by her every word, or more likely by her short shorts and skin-tight tee-shirt. Avoiding them, I took the long way around until I came to the spot where everybody had dumped their bags and belongings in a row on the grass.

I scanned the bleachers but didn't see Eli Fleming. Maybe he'd gotten the message yesterday that I didn't want him watching me. Before I dropped my bag on the ground, I pulled out a water bottle and took a long drink then capped it and tucked it back inside. Glancing up one more time, I saw a guy hiking up the bleachers two at a time, sunlight glinting off his long, brown hair. Jonah? I couldn't tell if it was him, but then he turned and waved at me. Jonah had come to watch me. *Oh, get over yourself. He might have come to watch somebody else.*

"I can't believe you showed up today," the taller-than-a-redwood girl said to me. She ditched her stuff next to mine. "I mean, I wouldn't have had the nerve."

I couldn't read her expression. Was it a, she's-got-guts look, or a she's-completely-clueless look? "Well, I promised Jazz." I hadn't, but it sounded good to blame somebody else for my stupidity.

"Hi, Lauren," Jazz said, flashing her pink braces smile and joining me in line. "I am glad you're here."

At least two people were happy to see me.

Jazz shielded her eyes and looked toward the bleachers. She waved at Jonah. "I told Jonah about yesterday, and he said he'd drop by today. He thought you might need to see a friendly face."

"H-H-Hey, Lauren," somebody called.

My stalker, Eli Fleming. He scuttled out onto the field, the only guy among dozens of girls. What was he doing? As if people weren't talking about me enough already.

Eli wore faded blue jeans ripped in both knees—the edges of the denim furry and frayed—and a wrinkled tee-shirt the color of algae. His anemic-white legs peeked through the holes in his pants.

He's just a lonely kid. Be nice. "Hey, Eli." I smiled even though I didn't feel like it.

"H-H-Hi, Lauren." He dropped his grungy backpack onto the ground and stooped to retrieve the dirty water bottle he'd offered me yesterday. "I brought you some water."

"You're sweet, but you don't need to bring me anything, OK?"

"Tiffany's heading over here," Jazz whispered.

"Wow, Lauren." Tiffany said. "Eli's so devoted to you. I wish I had a boyfriend who was into me so much."

"He is not her boyfriend." Jazz widened her stance and shoved her hands against her hips.

"Oh, OK. Whatever," Tiffany said. "By the way, Courtney's coming to school tomorrow. Just thought you'd want to know, so you can apologize to her."

"Sure," I said. "I'll tell her I'm sorry it happened."

"Want to know what she'll say?" Tiffany said. "Apology denied." She shoved me. I was too startled to react. "You have to pay for what you did."

*You have to pay for what you did...*I'd have to pay for the rest of my life for letting Haley die.

"If Courtney had been watching the ball, it never would have hit her in the face," Jazz said.

"Wrong, Miss Extra-Curricular. Lard Butt did it on purpose," Tiffany said. "So I'm thinking she should do Courtney's homework for, let's see, a month? Yeah, that seems fair."

You have to pay for what you did...

Along the sides of the field, distorted faces seemed to float, disembodied, jeering at me.

"Hey?" Tiffany snapped her fingers in front of my face. "You listening? You have to do her homework. For a month." She stood tall and confident, and the wind rippled her shoulder length hair like a flag caught in a breeze.

"Stop it," a voice said. And then an arm slid around my waist. Jonah's arm. Warm. Strong. Supporting me. When had he climbed down the bleachers?

"Oh, hey, Saint Jonah's here to rescue you,"

Tiffany said.

Jonah's arm tightened around me. He was so close. I could feel his breathing quicken and his muscles tense. "Leave her alone."

It wasn't a statement, it was a command...with an unspoken threat attached. Leave her alone or else...

"Whoa, calm down." Tiffany backed up a few steps.

"Y-Y-You OK, Lauren?" Eli asked moving beside us.

"Wow, Werthman, you're like a freak magnet," Tiffany said.

A whistle blew—one, two, three times. Miss Torrens strode out to where we were standing, the whistle bobbing against her chest, a deep frown creasing her forehead. "What's going on here?" This is girls' soccer conditioning." She eyed Eli and Jonah. "Why are you guys on the field?"

"Just came to watch my friends." Jonah removed his arm from around my waist.

"Is there a problem here, Miss Vancleave?" Miss Torrens asked.

Tiffany shook her head. "Nope." She sprinted over to the net and fell in line with some other girls.

Eli opened his mouth, on the verge of recounting the whole incident, but I shook my head.

"You ready to play goalie, Miss Werthman?" Miss Torrens asked.

So apparently she thought I was goalie material.

Candra thought I deserved to be happy.

Jonah said I should forgive myself.

They couldn't all be wrong, could they?

"She's ready." Jonah's fingertips brushed against mine on purpose, and shivers ran up my arm in spite of the warm temperature.

"See you after conditioning, OK?" He squeezed my hand and smiled.

I looked into those crystal blue eyes and I wanted to stay next to him forever. "OK," I whispered.

Jonah returned to the top bleacher, propped his feet on the seat ahead of him, and rested his hands on his knees. And Eli Fleming spun on his heel and tore off the field, heading for the parking lot.

Good. Maybe he'd leave me alone now.

"Nice stop, Werthman," Miss Torrens said when I caught the ball Jazz had kicked.

Whenever it was Tiffany's turn, she barreled for the ball full speed and kicked it as hard as she could, not at the net, but at me. Even with the goalie gloves on, my fingers stung from blocking her shots.

Conditioning lasted a little over an hour and I was exhausted, but I'd done a decent job.

"Ladies, over here," Miss Torrens said. "Same time tomorrow. I will post the list of girls who made the soccer team this Friday on the board right outside the gym. Oh, and I talked with Courtney Abrahms's mother today. Courtney's, fine, but she had to have a couple of stitches and she's dropping out of soccer. Good job, girls. Dismissed."

Stitches. They were never going to let me forget this.

19

Jazz invited me over after soccer conditioning, so I texted Dad and got his permission. She and I were lying on the floor in her room, staring at the ceiling, the door shut to "keep out the pest." Her mother had gone to the store, so she was babysitting her sister.

"I don't hear anything," I said with a growing sense of uneasiness. "Shouldn't you check on Tanvi?" I'd been in my room talking on my cell when Haley slipped out of the house.

"She is fine," Jazz said, seemingly unconcerned.

"How do you know she didn't go outside? Or that she's not messing with something dangerous?"

"Tanvi knows the rules. She is not allowed to go outside alone."

Neither was Haley. Adrenaline pumped through my body. I sat up, listening. Nothing. No cartoon voices on a television set. No little person voice. Tanvi wasn't playing with a doll or a toy, making it talk. Jazz didn't know what terrible things could happen when you weren't paying attention. "I really think we should check on her."

"Relax, OK? I've watched Tanvi lots of times before and trust me, she's fine."

"But what if—"

Someone tap-tap-tapped on the door.

"Go away, Tanvi! I am busy," Jazz hollered.

Thank God. Jazz sounded just like I used to sound.

Irritated. Tired of a pesky little sister disrupting her life. If she only knew…

"Too busy to speak with your mother? May I come in, please?"

"Sorry!" Jazz scrambled to open her door.

Mrs. Krishnan looked beautiful. She wore the traditional Indian sari in shades of orange, blue and yellow, accented with sparkly jewels. Her sleek hair was pulled back into a braid. "Jonah is here to see you," she said. "He's waiting in the kitchen."

"Oh, I forgot," Jazz said. "He told me he'd come over and help me with my math tonight."

"Good," I said. "I didn't understand the homework assignment either."

When we walked into the kitchen, Mrs. Krishnan was unpacking grocery bags, stacking canned goods in the cupboard.

Jonah was sitting cross-legged on the floor, wearing faded jeans, athletic shoes and a tie-dyed blue shirt that brought out the color of his eyes.

Tanvi faced him, a doll house between them, like the one my sister used to have. Dad donated it to the thrift shop along with most of her other toys, as if getting rid of her things would banish her from our thoughts.

Jonah knocked on the doll house door with the plastic dragon he had clutched in his hand. "Hey," he said in a gravelly voice, wiggling the dragon from side to side. "You need a fire-starter in there? I breathe the stuff out my nostrils, you know."

Mrs. Krishnan smiled.

Tanvi giggled and said, "I am not allowed to play with fire."

"But I am. Let me in."

"I don't think so, dragon. Go away." She walked her doll into the tiny kitchen and picked up a miniature phone, pretending to hit the speed-dial. "I'm calling the police. You'd better leave, dragon."

"No! Don't do that, little girl. I'm going." Jonah hopped the dragon away from the dollhouse door and grinned at us.

Dad used to play with Haley exactly the same way. When she had her dolls out, Dad would knock on the dollhouse with some ridiculous toy that didn't have anything to do with the dolls, and he'd make the toy talk in a silly voice. Haley adored it. She'd laugh until her stomach hurt.

"Lauren?" Jazz said.

I blinked. They were all staring at me. "Oh, sorry. I was just thinking about something."

"Must have been something serious," Jonah said.

The experts called it "baggage." Traumatic things that happened to you, leaving unseen scars, like wounds that never heal. What baggage did Jonah have? Or Jazz? Every family had secrets: A relative who drank too much. A Mom or Dad who gambled away their paycheck at the casino. Something.

Jonah fingered the cross around his neck. "You know, Lauren, whatever is bothering you, God already knows about it, and He will forgive you."

I sprang to my feet. "Oh, great! But here's the thing. I can't forgive Him, so why don't you just be quiet and leave me alone!" I shoved past him and hit the front door at a run.

"Wait," Mrs. Krishnan called. "Do you need a ride home?"

"No! I'm fine."

A few blocks later, I reached a small park and

dropped into a swing to catch my breath. The rubber seat molded itself around my hips and squeezed uncomfortably tight like a blood pressure cuff. I scuffed my shoe in the gravel.

"Lauren?" Jonah stepped from behind me, breathing hard.

He must have shot out of the Krishnans' house right behind me. Apparently Jesus Kids were taught to never to give up on a person. "Aren't you supposed to help Jazz with her math?" I asked.

"I'm not going back there unless you come with me." He sat on the swing next to mine. The seat was too low for him and his long legs stretched out.

"Then I guess you're not going back."

"OK with me. You're more important. Can I ask you a question?"

"Can I stop you?"

"No." He smiled. "Would you come with me Wednesday night to my youth group meeting at church?"

"No thanks." A person who killed her sister did not belong inside a church. If there was a God, He hated me, and I was certain He wouldn't want me inside His house. Besides, the feeling was mutual. The Head of the universe had the power to save my sister, but didn't.

"Everybody's nice. I promise, you'd have a good time. Come with me just once, and if you don't like it, I'll never bring it up again."

"I can't." The youth group meeting was probably like AA. I'd have to stand up in front of everybody and say something like, "Hi, my name is Lauren, and I'm a sinner." Christians believed in telling each other what they'd done wrong. Sharing their life stories. What'd they call them? Testimonies? What would I say? "I killed my little sister, but then I accepted Jesus, so now I'm happy again and I can go on living." What a lie. Jonah thought religion would cure me. He was wrong.

"Why are you so mad at God? Because it doesn't matter what you did, He still loves you."

Letting Haley die didn't matter? I pushed myself up out of the swing. "You don't know what you're talking about." I tried to run from him, but the gravel sucked at my shoes, pulling them down with every step, and made it impossible to move fast. When Jonah caught up with me, I shoved him, tried to get past him, but he wrapped his arms around me and pulled me close. His body felt good against mine, but feeling good made me uncomfortable. Why should I feel good when Haley was dead? It was wrong. I struggled to free myself.

"Tell me who you are," he said, his breath warm against my face. "I want to know everything about you."

"No, you don't. Let me go." But I didn't want him to let go. I was safe in his arms, and for a few minutes, all the bad stuff in my life disappeared. There was only this time and this place and the two of us. Jonah accepted me, baggage and all.

He reached out and brushed my hair away from my face. "I like you. I want to help."

"You can't. You can't take away what happened."

"I know, but you could talk about it, and it might help."

"If I told you, you'd hate me."

"I could never hate you." He leaned closer, and I looked into his amazing eyes, so bright, so full of optimism, and I believed him. Maybe I could tell him about Haley. A second later, his lips moved over mine. The kiss was warm and gentle and it felt like a thousand fireflies fluttered inside my stomach. I rested my head against his chest. The cross pendant pressed into my cheek.

"Why do you like me? I freak out daily. And I'm fat. What, do you like a challenge?"

"Shhh." Jonah hugged me, and I wrapped my arms around him.

We stood holding each other and swayed together next to the swing set. Neither of us said anything.

"Lauren!"

I flinched at the sound of Mom's voice. Jonah and I backed away from each other like we'd been tasered.

Mom had parked across the street, and the car's engine was still running.

"Your mom?" he whispered.

I nodded. My heart pounded hard. Heat washed over my face. Had she seen us kissing?

Mom rested her arm on the open car window and leaned forward, frowning. "I've been looking all over for you. Mrs. Krishnan called and said you left their house upset. That was over half an hour ago."

She was going to ground me forever.

"Get in the car, Lauren," Mom said. "Right now."

She completely ignored Jonah and he was standing right beside me. Worse, she'd just treated me like an eight-year-old in front of the boy who'd just kissed me.

Leave me alone! Too embarrassed to meet Jonah's eyes, I slipped into obedient child mode and walked to Mom's car, got in and slammed the door, never looking back.

For several blocks, Mom didn't say a word. She

just gripped the steering wheel in a choke hold, her lips frozen in a straight line, her forehead wrinkled. At the next intersection the light changed to red, and she braked and turned toward me. "Why didn't you answer your cell?"

I'd left it at Jazz's, along with my book bag, and the canvas bag that held my soccer shoes, shin guards, water bottle, and school clothes. *Way to go Lauren. She's already beyond mad, and now she'll rocket to totally ticked off.* I had to tell her, because I needed my things. "I forgot my stuff at Jazz's."

The light turned green. Mom drove through the intersection and parked along a tree-lined street, every house a boring shade of beige. "Are you kidding me?" she said. "First I worry myself sick wondering if you're all right, and now I have to drive back to the Krishnans' place?"

She was worried about me? I almost smiled, as crazy as it sounds, because if she was ready to kill me, it meant she still cared. "I'm sorry."

"You should be."

Ten minutes later, we were back in front of Jazz's.

"Hurry up," Mom said. "Your dad's waiting for us."

Mrs. Krishnan answered the door. "Hello, Lauren. Jazz, Lauren is here." After waving to my mother, she left the room.

Jazz came in, her arms weighed down with my bags, my cellphone clutched in her hand. "Here you go." She handed me everything.. "Did Jonah find you? He was really worried about you."

Two people were worried about me. "Yeah. At the park. I'm sorry I ran out of here."

She glanced at Mom's car. "Are you in trouble?"

Brenda Baker

"Big time." I thought about the way Jonah's lips had pressed against mine, warm and soft, and how incredible it felt to have his arms around me, and my mouth twitched into a crazy smile.

Jazz cocked her head, frowned. "Then why are you smiling?"

"Tell you tomorrow."

"Lauren, no! You have to tell me now."

"Sorry, I can't. Bye." I trucked back to our car, slinging my bags onto the backseat.

Mom and I rode in silence all the way home.

20

Dad followed us into the living room. He and Mom settled next to each other on the couch, not close together, but still, they formed a united front, ready to deal with their truant daughter.

I sat pillar-straight in the armchair facing them. I was so dead. Dead.

No, I wasn't dead. Haley might be gone forever, but I was very much alive.

Massaging her temples, Mom let out a sigh and shook her head. "You want to explain to me what you were doing at the park in the arms of some boy?"

Feeling better than I have in a long time. Jonah had kissed me, and I'd kissed him back.

"So she went to the park with a friend," Dad said. "What's the big deal?"

Like an eagle sizing up its prey, Mom turned and stared at Dad. "She was supposed to be at Kavya's. Then I get a phone call from Mrs. Krishnan, telling me our daughter ran out of their house, and a boy, whom we have never met, took off after her. You don't find that disturbing?"

"From what I understand, they're friends," Dad said.

The eagle narrowed her eyes. "Oh, they're much more than friends. Wait a second, you knew about this?"

"Lauren's mentioned Kavya and Jonah to me,

yes," Dad said evenly, not backing down from Mom's accusation.

"Can we please get back on track?" my mother asked. She folded her hands in her lap and narrowed her eyes again at me.

My parents were fighting as usual, but Mom was talking to Dad, not talking to him through me.

Dad reached for Mom's arm, and when his fingertips barely grazed the fabric of her shirt, she flinched. "Don't."

He retracted his hand, folded his arms over his chest, and cleared his throat. "Your mother asked you a question, Lauren. Answer her, please."

"Jonah really upset me so I left. Can I help it if he followed me?"

"This...Jonah? What did he say?" my mother asked.

I stared at my hands, wondering if I should tell her.

"Lauren?" Dad said. "Your Mom was worried. I think you owe her an explanation."

The smile twitched at my lips again. It wasn't funny, but in a way, it was, because I'd believed she'd be ecstatic if I dropped off the face of the earth.

"Jonah said...he said it didn't matter what I'd done, because God would forgive me."

"Oh, he's one of those." My mother crossed one leg over the other and bobbed it up and down impatiently. "A religious fanatic."

She had no right to call him names. "He's not a fanatic!"

Dad, in a diplomatic tone, cut in before Mom and I could launch into a full-scale war. "You haven't told him about your sister's accident?"

"No," I said. "I haven't told anybody. I thought we moved here to forget what happened."

"We will never forget Haley!" Mom said passionately. "Your father was insane to think we could move to a different state and pretend to only have one child."

"Lydia! What a terrible thing to say." The vein in Dad's neck pulsed.

The doorbell rang before Mom could reply.

Dad answered the door, and Jonah stood on the porch, thumbs hooked into the pockets of his jean shorts, sunlight glinting off the cross around his neck. "Mr. Werthman? I'm Jonah. Lauren's friend."

Mom craned her neck to get a closer look at the uninvited intruder, the boy who'd corrupted her daughter.

"This isn't a good time," Dad said in a low voice. "Lauren's busy."

Mom sprang off the couch. "No, no, no. Have him come in. I think it's better if we talk to both of them."

Standing aside, Dad motioned for Jonah to enter.

Grim-faced, glancing first at me and then at my mother, Jonah looked nervous, like a kid who hadn't studied for a big exam and knew he was about to flunk.

I wanted to bolt out of my chair and tell him everything would be fine, but no way was that happening, because Mom looked ready to skip the jury and go right to the sentencing.

"So, Jonah, is it?" Mom said. "What are you doing here?"

"I came to apologize."

"Have a seat," Dad said.

"I'll stand, thanks." Jonah crossed the room and

stopped beside my chair. "You shouldn't blame Lauren for this. It was my fault she ran out of the Krishnans' house. I came here because I didn't want her to get into trouble."

"How very noble," Mom said, "but I'm afraid you're too late. Lauren's already in trouble. There is something you can do, though."

Jonah's face brightened. "Name it."

"Leave my daughter alone. Her life is complicated enough right now. She doesn't need a boyfriend, especially one who preaches to her about God."

"Mom!" How could she? I jumped out of my chair.

"Mrs. Werthman," Jonah said. "We're just friends."

"Do you think I'm stupid, young man?" Mom said. "I saw you."

Jonah fisted his hands. "No! You don't understand."

"Let's all calm down," Dad said. "Anybody want something to drink?" He glanced at me, as if realizing what he'd said, and I knew we were both thinking the same thing—Mom probably wanted a drink in the worst way.

"Oh, I understand perfectly," Mom said. "I've known people like you, people who leaf through their Bibles and memorize scripture so they can fling words at you when something unthinkable happens."

Sweat broke out on Jonah's forehead. He reached into his pocket and produced a squishy ball, his hand tightening around it, squeezing and releasing, over and over. Mom was getting to him. She was getting to all of us.

"What are you doing?" Mom eyed the ball. "Some kind of anger management?"

Jonah's cheeks reddened. "It's nothing," he said, stuffing the ball out of sight.

"Maybe you'd better go," Dad said to Jonah.

"Yeah, maybe I should." Jonah hurried to the door, relief evident on his face. He wanted to leave, and Dad had just given him an out.

"How'd you get here?" Dad asked.

Jonah paused, his hand on the doorknob. "I rode my bike."

"Well, where do you live?" Dad asked.

"Ninety-ninth and Maple."

"That's a long way from here." Dad joined Jonah at the door. "Lauren and I will give you a ride home. We can throw your bike into the back of my truck."

Thanks, Dad. At least I had one reasonable parent. I stood.

But Mom executed a block better than any defensive lineman. "Lauren's not going anywhere with that boy," she said.

Dad held a hand up to stop her from saying more. "Kids, can you give us a minute, please? Wait outside, OK?"

We stepped onto the front porch, but it wasn't hard to hear what Dad said to her, because he screamed it: "Don't you ever say anything like that again! Haley was my child too, and I will miss her for the rest of my life!"

There it was. The truth. Out in the open for Jonah to examine. He now knew I'd had a sister, and he'd want to know what happened to her.

Jonah's fingers curled around mine. "I'm so sorry, Lauren."

I squeezed his hand. He pulled me close and I rested my head against his chest. The steady thrum of his heartbeat whispered in my ear.

When Dad flung open the door, Mom wasn't right behind him like I'd expected. Their fight must have stopped her from charging outside and forbidding me to ride along.

"You guys ready to go?" Dad asked, taking in the scene—Jonah holding me in his arms—and then gazing at the ground. To Dad's credit, he didn't mention it.

After brushing his fingertips over my hair, Jonah let go of me. "Yeah, Mr. Werthman, thanks."

Together Jonah and Dad hoisted his bike into the truck bed, and we piled inside the cab. Tuning the radio to his favorite oldies channel, Dad sang along, not hitting a single note right. Unfortunately, he knew the words to every song the station played, so we had to listen to his off-key concert the entire trip.

Most of the houses in Jonah's neighborhood needed a makeover, including a fresh coat of paint to cover their faded colors, and somebody to chop down the weeds—the only thing thriving in their front yards.

"Thanks again, Mr. Werthman," Jonah said. His house had a handicap ramp leading to a scarred wooden door, various toys strewn on the grass—a bike with training wheels, a plastic bucket and shovel, a deflated ball—and a chain staked into the ground with no dog attached to the end.

"You're welcome, Jonah."

"See you tomorrow in school, Lauren."

I nodded. Who was handicapped in his family? Why didn't he talk about having brothers or sisters? Clearly younger kids lived here too. Apparently, I wasn't the only one with secrets.

21

Second period, hyperventilating because I was expecting Jonah to search for me before lunchtime, I rushed into Candra's deserted office and considered hiding under her desk for the rest of the day. But with my luck, somebody would report me, and I'd wind up in Hazzardville again. Her desktop, usually cluttered with files, empty pop cans, and post-it notes, looked abandoned, as did the rest of the space except for Harley, who cowered in the corner of his cage.

Terrified, he shivered as if I had "squash the hamster" thoughts on my mind. "It's OK, buddy." I grabbed the hamster food, raised Harley's cage door, and shook pellets into his empty dish. He scurried onto his exercise wheel and ran in frenzied circles. Was he trying to escape from me? I was *not* going to sing "Twinkle, Twinkle Little Star" to a hamster, 'cause if anybody walked past the door and heard me, it would prove I was crazy.

Day one without Candra, and Harley and I missed her crazy bad. I stuck my hand in my pocket, felt the business card with her cell number, and was tempted to call, but it wasn't right to bother her while she was away.

There was so much I needed to tell her. About Haley. About Jonah. About me getting in trouble with Mom and Dad. How ironic. I was ready to tell Candra everything, but she wasn't here.

I refilled Harley's water container and replaced it

on the side of his cage. Mr. Bixby was expecting me. "See you tomorrow. Don't worry, buddy, you'll be fine."

"And so will you," Candra would say. "Now go do your student aide gig." I smiled, picturing her at her desk, legs propped up, hoop earrings dangling to her jaw line, a trio of silver bracelets on each arm.

But I didn't feel fine. I had to go to the main office and sit on display while I helped the staff do...what? I had no idea what a student aide did. And then later, I'd have to face Jonah and answer his questions about Haley. I needed chocolate to make it through the day. In five minutes, I could slip into a restroom and eat a few mini bars...

"The next time you want to binge eat, write down what you're feeling instead. Then wait a few minutes, and the urge will probably pass."

Candra was gone, but in a way, she was with me. Everything she'd told me, everything we'd talked about, ran through my mind constantly. Dropping into the chair I always sat in, I pulled the spiral notebook out of my book bag and wrote: "I feel...alone, scared, worried. What will Jonah think of me when he hears the whole story? I am MAD at my mother. She embarrassed me and treated Jonah with a complete lack of respect."

When I glanced up at the clock, three minutes had passed, and my chocolate craving hadn't budged. All I could think about was how rich, gooey, and satisfying the candy would taste, and how eating chocolate would calm me down.

"H-H-Hi, Lauren." Eli's lanky frame filled the doorway. A fresh pimple colony populated his face. His eyes were a bit bloodshot, like he hadn't slept much last night.

"Hey." I did not need this today. Why me? It was like I had a sign taped to my back: "Attention all weird, freaky people. I'll be your friend."

"W-W-Where's Miss Gladden?"

"Out of town. I'm taking care of her hamster this week."

Eli looked almost normal today, wearing an unstained blue tee-shirt and rip-free jeans, but his sneakers were faded and a patch of white sweat sock showed through the thin canvas on his right shoe.

The chocolate crunch bars in my book bag were whispering my name. "Well, I have to go."

Eli backed up letting me past. "I'll, um, walk with you. Where are you going?"

None of your business. "The office." He didn't need to know I'd be there every day this week. I walked faster, hoping he'd get the message to leave me alone.

"Oh. D-D-Did you get the math assignment done?"

"Yeah, look, I'm in a hurry, so I'll see you later, OK?" I veered into a restroom before he could reply.

"Oh, God," a girl said.

Tiffany's voice. She was on her knees—definitely not praying—in front of a toilet. The smell of vomit mingled with the normal bathroom odor. Breathing through my mouth, I ditched my book bag, rushed to the locked door and knocked on it. "Tiffany? What's the matter?"

"Lauren? Is that you? I'm sick. I feel like I might pass out."

"I'll get help." She called me Lauren...The girl must really be sick.

"No! Are you crazy? You can't tell anybody!"

She was in there throwing up, ready to faint, and she was calling me crazy? "Then what do you want me to do?"

"I'll be OK. Just give me a minute. If anybody comes in, act normal. Don't tell them anything. Promise me."

"Tiffany, I really think—"

"I don't care what you think!" She sobbed. "Ow…it hurts when I breathe."

Not good. Mr. Bixby would wonder where I was, but I couldn't leave her alone. "Open the door."

"I can't. I'm dizzy."

After a couple of minutes, the stall door squealed open and Tiffany emerged, her mascara smudged, her lips pale, and her hair, usually perfect, now a tangled mess. Her tee-shirt was stained and wrinkled. She took three shaky steps, gasping, and had to lean against the wall for support. The knuckles on her right hand were bruised.

How'd she get the bruises? With black mascara beneath both eyes, she looked bizarre, like a rabid raccoon. "You're having trouble breathing?"

"Yeah. But if you mention this to anyone, you're dead."

But if I don't tell someone, you might be dead. "I have to get to the office. I'm a student aide this week for Mr. Bixby." But first, I'm getting the nurse.

"Go ahead, I'm fine now."

But she wasn't.

Her knees buckled and she crumpled to the floor like a wilted flower, her head clunking against the hard tiles, her legs splaying out sideways.

"Tiffany!" I shook her, but she didn't respond. Oh, God. What should I do? Why did catastrophe strike people when I was around?

This isn't about you. See if she's breathing. With trembling fingers, I touched her neck to check for a pulse, relieved when I found one. How hard had she hit her head? There was no blood on the floor which was a good thing.

Should I leave her and run for help? What if she quit breathing while I was gone? "Tiffany!" Cradling her head with one hand, I shook her arm again. She wouldn't wake up.

And then I remembered another horrible day, the day I heard my mother scream. I ran outside and found her kneeling over Haley, doing CPR. My sister's hair was wet, her skin beaded with water, glistening in the sun. She'd jumped into our pool, and she wasn't breathing.

I stooped beside my mother and tapped one of Haley's pale, skinny arms. "Wake up, Haley! Wake up!" *You can't die. You can't.*

Mom quit pumping Haley's chest. "Stop it, Lauren! Go call 911. Then call your dad." She counted compressions again, and then tried to breathe life into Haley.

This isn't Haley; it's Tiffany and you have to do something.

I stumbled to the restroom door and shoved it open. "Help!"

No teachers were patrolling the hallway. No students. They were all in class. Nobody heard me. But then I saw someone at the far end of the hall, just coming out of a restroom.

"Hey! Help!"

The kid jerked his head around. Eli. He sprinted toward me on his gangly legs, bony arms pumping,

over-sized feet thudding against the linoleum floor—
and stopped, breathless right in front of me. "L-L-
Lauren? What's the matter?"

"Get the nurse. Hurry!"

The pupils in his pea-green eyes dilated, worry
colored his face. "Are you sick?"

"No, it's Tiffany."

"W-W-Where is she?" He peered through the
propped open door.

"In here. Please go!"

"O-O-OK. His sneakers screeched against the floor
as he disappeared around the corner.

I flew back inside the restroom to check on
Tiffany.

She stirred, and then she opened her eyes, looking
groggy. "What happened?"

"You passed out. How do you feel?"

Slowly, she sat, rubbing her forehead. "My head
hurts."

"Does it still hurt to breathe?"

"No, that's gone now." Grasping the edge of a
sink, she pulled herself to a standing position and
glanced in the mirror. "I look awful," she said, finger-
combing her flyaway hair. Snatching a paper towel
from the dispenser, she dabbed at the raccoon smudges
under her eyes.

She was worried about how she looked?
Unbelievable. "Maybe you should eat something."

Whirling around, her eyes narrowed, and she
opened her mouth to yell at me, but she was shaky and
had to grab the sink to keep her balance.

"If you're dizzy, you should sit and put your head
between your knees."

"Thank you, Dr. Lauren."

Ah, she was back, the Tiffany we all knew and hated. "You scared me. People don't fall down unconscious for no reason."

She smoothed make-up under her eyes and patted blusher on her cheeks. "Here's a thought. Go away and forget you ever saw me."

I threw my hands in the air, and let my arms slap against my sides. "You're welcome, Tiffany. Geesh. I try to help you, and you're still incredibly rude to me."

"I didn't ask for your help, did I?" She drew a deep breath, still clutching the sink for support.

A loud pounding on the restroom door made us both jump. "Lauren? It's Mr. Bixby. The nurse is with me. We're coming in."

Tiffany's head swiveled toward me and her mouth dropped open, her eyes wide. "What did you do, Werthman?"

22

The nurse, a pudgy middle-aged woman with wispy brown hair, touched Tiffany's arm. "You think you can walk to my office?" she asked. "Or do you need to sit in the wheelchair?"

"Wheelchair?" Tiffany's stare scorched through me. "I'm fine. I skipped breakfast, so I guess it made me dizzy."

Mr. Bixby frowned, folded his arms over his chest and leaned against the wall, shaking his head. "Tiffany, fainting is not an everyday occurrence. Lauren said you were unconscious for several minutes, so it's best to err on the side of caution, don't you agree?"

Should I tell them Tiffany had thrown up? That it had happened before? Not unless I had a death wish, because Tiffany would lunge for my throat if I said anything. But something was seriously wrong with her.

"Look," Tiffany said, "Lauren jumped to the wrong conclusion." She smiled her room brightening smile, the one that turned boys into putty. "She shouldn't have sent for you."

The nurse stared at the bruises on Tiffany's knuckles, until Tiffany noticed and plunged both hands into the pockets of her jeans.

"I think you'd better come with me," the nurse said.

Grabbing the arms of the wheelchair, the nurse

rolled it to the door and nudged it open with the toe of her white leather shoe.

Eli, who must have been standing too close, jumped out of the way, nearly getting knocked over by the door.

"Excuse me," the nurse said gruffly.

We filed out of the restroom behind her—Tiffany, me, and Mr. Bixby—one strange-looking parade. Whenever we passed a classroom, heads turned to stare at us, and Tiffany's face shaded a deeper red.

"Is she, um, OK?" Eli asked, bumbling along beside me.

"What's he doing here?" Tiffany scrunched up her nose as if a stink bomb had exploded in the hallway.

"He got the nurse," I said.

"Great, Fleming," Tiffany said, sarcasm peppering her words. "Thanks a lot."

Eli's head drooped. His shoulders caved in, and his steps became tentative.

"Hey," I said to him, "Thanks for helping me out." For once I was glad he'd been lurking nearby.

His posture straightened and a broad smile spread across his face. "Y-Y-You're welcome."

"Eli," Mr. Bixby said, "We appreciate what you did, but why don't you go on to class now?"

"S-S-Sure." Eli beamed. "I'll see you later, Lauren."

"Yeah, later." I was grateful, a word I never thought I'd associate with Eli Fleming, but he was there for me when I needed somebody.

When we reached the nurse's office, Mr. Bixby said to her, "Please keep me informed."

"Certainly," she said. A row of plastic chairs lined the wall outside her doorway. "Lauren, could you please wait out here while I talk to Tiffany?"

"OK." I slouched into a chair, glad to see they were the kind without arms so I wouldn't have to wedge myself in. The longer I spent there, the less time I had to spend being a student aide.

"I'll need to call your parents," the nurse said to Tiffany.

"Why?" She half whined, half shrieked. "I feel fine."

"School policy." The nurse ushered her through the door and closed it behind them.

Their conversation was muffled, but I caught a few words:

"Dieting?" the nurse's voice.

"Not hungry." Tiffany's voice.

"Binge eating—" the nurse said.

Tiffany binged? I'd seen her tray in the cafeteria. She ate nothing but freebies, the word my mother used for food that wouldn't make you fat—fruits and vegetables like lettuce, carrot sticks, and apples.

"Dangerous," the nurse said. "People die."

"I don't do that!" Tiffany said.

The door creaking open startled me. "Lauren, would you mind waiting with Tiffany? I'm going to grab her something to eat from the cafeteria."

Like she wanted me, the traitor, to stay with her. I stood and hesitated in the doorway.

"Be back as soon as I can," the nurse said, her shoes squeaky against the polished faux stone flooring.

"Come on in, Werthman," Tiffany said. "Join the party."

Right. Her voice sounded flat, and she was about as enthusiastic as somebody at a funeral.

The room smelled like disinfectant. I sat in one of

the teal chairs arranged in front of the window. Sunlight shone through white mini-blinds, and slanted rays fell across Tiffany, who was lying on a bed topped with a plastic mattress and a white paper sheet. She propped herself up on one elbow. "Why'd you have to butt in? I am so screwed because of you."

You're welcome. I could have left you passed out on the bathroom floor! Counting to ten, I took a deep breath. "If that was a thank you, it needs work."

Tiffany swung her legs onto the floor and sat. "You expect me to be grateful?" She stood, model-walked to a tall glass-fronted cabinet balanced along the opposite wall, and yanked the cabinet door open, absently fiddling with the lids on the clear glass containers holding tongue depressors, Q-tips, and bandages. "Don't hold your breath, Werthman."

"My mother hangs out at the gym every day, but she always carries her cell," Tiffany said, "and unfortunately, the school had her number on file. I think Mom's session with her personal trainer got interrupted which will be the first thing to tick her off, and I'll be the second."

"What was I supposed to do? Leave you there unconscious?"

One of the glass containers in the cabinet toppled over and Tiffany quickly righted it and replaced the contents before closing the cupboard door. "No, but you didn't have to go blabbing to the nurse and the principal and that freak, Eli. And now my mother's on her way here. Do you have any idea how difficult my mother is to deal with?"

"Well, if she's anything like mine, then yeah."

Tiffany and I stared at each other for several seconds.

"Why do you do it?" I asked her. "Make yourself throw up?"

She crossed her legs, seemed to consider my question. "A couple of years ago, I was fat," she said. "And I'm never letting myself get fat again."

"You?"

"I know, right? My parents split up, and I started eating everything in sight. Whole cartons of ice cream. Chocolate. Cookies. Donuts. I craved sugar constantly."

Sounded just like me. Food was my best friend. It could raise my mood in mere seconds. "You have to stop throwing up. It's dangerous."

"Look, Lauren, I know you're like this Good Samaritan or something, since you hang out with Jonah, but it's my life, OK?"

Was that why I helped her? Were Jonah's beliefs seeping into my subconscious? No, the old me would have helped her too. It was how my parents raised me, to care about other people. Didn't Tiffany realize life was fragile? You could be here, making plans for the day, the week, the year, and next thing you know, bam, your life is erased like it never mattered at all. Like my sister. "You think the nurse will tell your mother?"

Tiffany unzipped her purse, uncapped a small bottle of breath freshener, and spritzed some in her mouth. "Duh, yes. But she has no proof, and you won't say anything, right?"

"Did the nurse say you could die?" Was Tiffany bulimic? I'd heard of it, but never knew anybody who had it.

She waved me off. "They always tell you the worst case scenario. That'll never happen to me." Stepping through an open doorway leading to a small bathroom, she checked her reflection in the mirror on the wall. "I know what I'm doing." She dabbed more make-up under her eyes and ran a brush through her hair. "How do I look?"

"Good, actually." You couldn't tell less than fifteen minutes ago, this girl had been sick and lying unconscious on the bathroom floor.

"Thanks."

"I still think you should get some help before something else bad happens."

"Nothing bad will happen. I've been doing this for a long time. You know, you're not much different than me."

"I guess not. Except I'd never do what you do."

Tiffany looked toward the door. "The nurse is coming back. One question. Why did you stay with me? You don't even like me."

"Anybody would have done the same thing."

The nurse returned and handed Tiffany a cup of yogurt. "Here you are. Finish it all."

Tiffany smiled, took the yogurt and spoon and said, "Thanks," looking directly at me.

23

Mrs. Burns, the school secretary, ushered me to a desk facing her own, perfectly arranged, everything in its place. "Sit here, and I'll find you something to do." She removed her glasses and they dangled from a silver, little-old-lady chain fastened around her wrinkled neck.

Ugh. Every day, second period for the next week, I'd have a front row seat watching this woman with skin stretched tight over her skeletal frame, and her blue-veined hands, withered like prunes. I would be so glad to see Candra when she got back.

Still, the student aide gig was better than going to gym class. Plus, I had a great view of the fish tank, its green plants, hula dancers swaying in the clear water, and black fish darting in and out of the castle on the rocky bottom. The pump hummed as bubbles floated to the surface. If I concentrated on the fish tank, I could avoid seeing the fluorescent lights that flooded the office with too bright artificial light, the kind you saw in hospital emergency rooms, the kind that made you feel cold the instant you walked in.

Just then Mr. Bixby strode out of his office, his steps bouncy, purposeful; a man on a mission. "Oh, Lauren, good, you're here. When Tiffany's mother arrives, would you please take her to the nurse's office?" He checked his watch. "She should be here in a few minutes. Bring her and Tiffany to my office, OK?"

"Sure." Would Mrs. Vancleave ask me any questions? She might, since I was the one to find Tiffany. Well, I'd give her the facts, but leave out the one about finding Tiffany kneeling in front of the toilet.

"Here we go." Mrs. Burns laid a stack of papers on my desk. Alongside the papers, she placed a shallow dish with a sponge island in the middle, and a stamp dispenser. "First, you fold the letter into thirds," she said, "like so." Her ghostly white hands moved so fast, I could hardly follow. "Then, you stuff the letters in the envelopes, run the flap over the wet sponge and seal it. When you're finished, drop the letters in the out-box here."

"Got it," I said. It wouldn't take long. The stack of paper wasn't thick.

But then Mrs. Burns pulled more from a cardboard box beneath her desk. Now the stack looked as deep as the package of paper Mom bought for our printer at home.

"There are three hundred letters. That ought to keep you busy." She smiled, her yellowish teeth on display.

I glanced at the black-framed clock on the wall. Yeah, I'd keep busy, considering there were only fifteen minutes left in second period, and it would take me twice the time it had taken her to fold each letter.

A woman rushed in, wearing an expensive-looking zip front warm-up suit, leather sneakers, and diamond stud earrings. Her hair was blonde, except for the roots, which had traces of brown. "Where's the nurse's office?" she asked.

"Mrs. Vancleave?" Mrs. Burns said. The woman nodded. "This is Lauren. She'll take you there."

A tight smile flickered across the woman's lips. "Thank you. Lead the way."

It felt weird to be the one in charge, the one who knew the way, especially since an adult was following me.

The jog suit swished as Mrs. Vancleave walked. "Mr. Bixby told me another student found my daughter. Do you know who?"

Well, what was I supposed to do, lie? "Yeah, actually, it was me. I asked a boy to get the nurse."

"Thank you, Lauren. Tiffany skips meals, and she complains about her weight all the time, but I don't understand why, because the girl doesn't have an ounce of fat on her."

She didn't understand a lot of things, but I hoped, for Tiffany's sake, the nurse would enlighten her.

When we reached the nurse's office, Tiffany was sprawled across the paper-lined bed, a white washcloth over her eyes. She heard us come in and sat up, swinging her legs over the side of the bed. "Hi, Mom."

"I'll bet you haven't had anything to eat all day," her mother said. "How many times do I have to tell you to eat something?"

Wow. She didn't bother to say hello or even ask if Tiffany was feeling better. Her mother was a lot like mine, only the message was reversed: eat, versus stop eating.

The nurse, who'd been sitting behind her desk, pushed her chair back and stood. She walked over to Mrs. Vancleave and then turned to me. "Thank you, Lauren, you can go."

"Mr. Bixby asked me to bring them back to the office," I said.

"I'll handle it," the nurse said. "I need to talk to Mrs. Vancleave."

"OK." This was between the three of them. "Hope you feel better, Tiffany."

"I'm fine."

I nodded and left the room.

24

My cell rang just as Jazz and I were climbing the bus steps. "Hello?"

"Lauren? It's Dad. Where are you?"

His voice sounded strange, as if he was trying to stay calm, but I caught the undertone of urgency. "Just getting on the bus. What's wrong?"

Jazz's gaze met mine, and concern flashed in her dark eyes.

"Get off and wait for me out front. I'll pick you up in ten minutes."

What now? I didn't need any more drama in my life. "Dad, you're scaring me. Tell me what's going on."

"It's your mother. There's been an accident."

No, no, no! "What kind of accident? How bad?"

"Listen, honey. We need to get to the hospital now. I'll fill you in on the way."

"OK." I hit the end button on my cell, and turned to fight my way through the pack of students boarding the bus. Kids yelled, "Watch it," and "Hey, quit pushing," but I didn't care what they thought. I had to get off the bus immediately.

I felt a tug on my arm.

"Lauren?" Jazz said. "Wait! Where you going?"

"Hospital. It's my mom."

"What happened?" Jazz shouted above the rising

chaos around us.

The bus driver hollered at kids to take a seat.

Students laughed, their voices on high volume.

"My dad said there was an accident. That's all I know."

"Call me," she said as I finally reached the bottom of the stairs.

An accident. Our family couldn't handle another accident.

I sat on edge of the huge, concrete block planter in the middle of the courtyard waiting for Dad. Above me, the flag whipped in the breeze. The wood mulch smelled freshly spread. It covered the ground surrounding the flagpole, cushioning the flowering bushes from weeds. I scanned the road for Dad's truck, but school buses clogged the road end to end, blocking my view. Maybe I should wait up by the buses. If he parked on the opposite side of the street, I'd miss him.

"Hey, Lauren." Jonah, wearing jeans frayed at the bottoms and a faded tie-died tee-shirt, strode toward me, an easy smile flickering across his face, until he got closer and saw my expression. "Something wrong?"

Students streamed from the building.

Teachers hustled toward the staff parking lot, juggling laptop cases and canvas bags.

Do not lose it. Not here. Not in front of everybody. "My dad's picking me up." There. Maybe he'd drop it and I wouldn't have to explain, because tears were already blurring my vision.

He sat beside me and draped an arm over my shoulders. "Come on. I know you. Something's up. Talk to me."

I could smell his shampoo and cologne. I wanted to stay here with Jonah and pretend everything was fine so I wouldn't have to face whatever it was I had to face at the hospital. *Just wait with me. Don't make me say anything. Please.*

The sun broke free from behind a cloud.

Jonah squeezed my arm. "It's OK. You don't have to tell me," he said, as if he'd read my mind. Gently, he pulled my head toward his shoulder and I leaned against him, feeling stronger because he was there.

A horn honked, and my dad leaned out the truck window. "Lauren. Come on!"

"Later," I said, jumping to my feet. "I have to go."

"What can I do?" Jonah called.

"Find Jazz. She knows what's happening," I yelled over my shoulder, sprinting for the truck.

Dad barely mumbled a hello and he didn't smile at me. Stubble shadowed his chin. His shirt was wrinkled as if he'd slept in it. Turning the wheel sharply, he peeled away from the curb, tires screeching, and sped up the street. The radio wasn't tuned to the oldies channel; it wasn't even on.

My pulse raced. "Dad? What happened?"

"She was driving on a gravel road outside the city, and they think she lost control of the car and rolled it into a ditch."

What was she doing there? "Will she be OK?"

"I don't know, honey. The police called and told me to go straight to Mercy Hospital."

How seriously was she hurt? Could she die? How could this be happening to us again?

I think Dad broke every speed law. We made it to the hospital in under ten minutes and checked in at the emergency room entrance.

"Lydia Werthman," Dad said. "Can we see her?"

"I'm sorry," the admittance clerk said. "They're

still treating her. If you'll take a seat, someone will be out to talk to you as soon as possible."

"But how is she?" Dad's voice was high-pitched, borderline hysterical.

"You'll have to ask the attending physician." The woman's gaze returned to the computer screen in front of her and her fingers danced across the keyboard.

I clenched my fists and slammed them against the check-in desk. "I want to see my mother!"

The admittance clerk looked startled and stared up at us. "Sir, please. I know you're both worried, but all you can do for now is wait."

"Come on." Dad touched my arm and steered me toward the waiting area. We sank into stiff-backed chairs, and I glanced at the ceiling-mounted TV where a newscaster was reporting the latest gloom and doom from around the world.

I closed my eyes and sagged against my dad, remembering the last time we'd waited in a hospital emergency room. Haley had been brought there by ambulance. Mom rode with Haley. They couldn't keep her away. When Dad and I got to the hospital, the admittance clerk told us to sit down until a doctor came to talk to us.

Mom had come through the doors first, a nurse supporting her by the arm. "They wouldn't let me stay with her," she said to us. "They should have let me stay!"

"It's OK, honey," Dad said.

The nurse gestured toward a private room. "Why don't you wait in there?" she said.

It was the kind of room they took you to when they had bad news to deliver, so when you cried out and screamed and fell apart, no one else had to watch.

Dad, me, and Mom huddled close together inside the room, waiting for some doctor we didn't know to change our whole world.

I still remembered feeling hopeful, thinking even though the situation might be bad, everything would eventually be OK. Like maybe Haley was in a coma, but she'd come out of it.

"We did everything we could," the doctor had said, "but in spite of our best efforts, we weren't able to save Haley. I'm sorry." He delivered these words as if he were reciting a play script, a memorized speech, and we weren't the first people to hear it.

He was sorry? Doctors were supposed to help people weren't they? It was a mistake. A huge mistake. He'd gotten Haley mixed up with another little girl. Five-year-olds did not die.

"I'll send someone else in to talk with you about what happens next," the doctor said. And then he'd turned away from us, ready to leave us there, stunned and broken.

"Wait! Where is she?" I said. "I want to see her." If I could just touch her, feel the warmth of her skin then none of it would be real.

"Honey, no, not now," Dad said.

"Someone will be with you shortly." The doctor walked briskly to the door and closed it behind him.

"Noooo." A low moan escaped from my mother's lips. She was shaking and she slumped down, and Dad had to catch her before she crashed against the floor and shattered into pieces like broken glass.

The sound of the door whooshing open brought me back to the present. I raised my head to see who was coming inside—Jonah, his hair mussed, the nail cross bobbing against his tee-shirt as he walked over to us.

Dad stared blankly as if he didn't know him, but then recognition registered in his eyes. "What are you doing here?" he asked.

"Mr. Werthman, I hope you don't mind, but I heard what happened and I wanted to stay with Lauren. I thought maybe I could help."

Yes. Stay. Just having you here makes me feel better.

Dad slowly shook his head. "There's nothing you can do."

"Please, Dad. Can he wait with us?"

Dad patted my leg and offered a weak smile. "Sure, honey." He sat hunched inside his baggy clothes like a turtle retreating inside its shell.

Jonah reached into his pocket and pulled out some coins. "How 'bout some coffee? Lauren, do you want a soda?"

"Coffee sounds good," Dad said mechanically, eyeing the right hand corner of the room where a counter held an empty coffee pot, packets of tea, sugar and creamer. "One sugar, no cream, please."

Reaching for my hand, Jonah pulled me out of my chair. "Good. We'll be right back. I saw a machine down the hall."

I let Jonah lead me away from Dad, away from the agonizing waiting room, around a corner to a vending machine. He fed some coins into the slot, a cup dropped into the open window, and the smell of fresh-brewed coffee filled the air. "What kind of soda do you want?" he asked, plugging more coins into the machine.

I touched A-7 and a can banged into the receptacle. "I don't want to go back."

He touched my face. "I know."

25

Jonah and I returned to the waiting room, him carrying two cans of pop, me carrying Dad's coffee and a packet of sugar.

Dad and a white-coated doctor were huddled together in a corner talking. That was good, right? Because the doctor hadn't called Dad into one of those private rooms.

But I couldn't shake the feeling something was terribly wrong, and when Dad glanced my way, I read the confirmation in his eyes—a look of defeat and a sickening sadness. My hand trembled so badly I had to give the coffee cup to Jonah so I wouldn't spill it.

"Go," Jonah whispered.

My legs felt wooden as I crossed the room. Late afternoon sunrays beamed through the windows and a disinfectant smell hung in the air. Fluorescent ceiling lights made the space a dizzying white. A musical jingle sang from the wall-mounted TV. When I stopped beside my dad, he tried to reassure me with a smile, but it was so fake, I felt even more scared. What was left of my family was sinking, and all I could do was cling to a tiny life-preserver of hope. "How's Mom?"

Before Dad could say anything, the doctor extended his hand, his fingers long and slender, the nails scrubbed clean. "You must be Lauren," he said. No smile from Doctor Clean Nails, just the familiar, oh-you-poor-kid look.

I shook his hand, more from reflex than good manners, because numbness had settled over me like paralysis, the kind that comes when you've heard bad news too many times.

"Your mom has some lacerations," the doctor said, "and she was unconscious when the other motorist found her. As I was explaining to your dad, we'd like to keep her overnight for observation. It'll be a few minutes before you can see her, because the police are questioning her right now."

"The police?" I blurted out, turning to Dad. "Why are the police talking to Mom?" Dread twisted in my stomach sharper than the cramps you get from the stomach flu. I was afraid I knew the answer, but Mom wouldn't drink and drive, would she? Why not? She'd been drinking all the time lately.

"Thank you, doctor," Dad said. "I'll take it from here."

After shaking Dad's hand, Doctor Clean Nails nodded and ambled away, his green over-the-shoe booties soundless against the white tiles.

Jonah watched from across the room, but he didn't come over. He leaned back against the wall, crossed his arms, and lowered his chin to his chest as if this wasn't any of his business, and he didn't want to interrupt our private conversation.

I wished something would interrupt it. Anything. Maybe if I concentrated hard enough, an ambulance would come roaring into the garage, and the doctors and nurses would have to snap into action and treat the victims. Then I could put off asking Dad the question I didn't want to ask. Biting my lip, I swallowed and muttered, "Was Mom drinking?"

Dad turned toward me and put his hands on my

shoulders, pivoting me to face him. "Lauren, honey…" he said, in his softest voice, "I don't know for sure."

But he suspected it. I could tell. Suddenly I had the urge to burst through the double doors, find my mother and yell at her: "You're so stupid! How could you do this? You could have killed yourself."

Dad clasped my hand, studied the floor for a couple seconds, then looked into my eyes again. "It could have been worse. She didn't hurt anyone else."

But she could have.

"She needs us now. We have to—"

I raised a hand to stop him. "No! Don't." Out of the corner of my eye, I saw Jonah heading our way. Shrugging out of Dad's grasp, I barreled to the garage entrance.

"Lauren, wait!" Dad yelled.

"Let me talk to her," Jonah said.

Leaves crunched under my feet as I ran. Was Jonah's God still punishing me? Why didn't He just take me out and end all our misery? At the outer edge of the parking lot, I stopped under a tree that had shed half its leaves, its bare branches waving in the wind like bony skeleton fingers. Leaning against the rough bark, I slid to the ground onto a carpet of brown leaves, not caring as the tree trunk snagged my shirt and bit into my back.

I looked up. Airplane contrails formed puffy white X's in the sky. Was God beyond the clouds somewhere, considering his next move to ruin my life? Was the earth His giant chessboard, and we were just pawns sacrificed in some twisted game?

"What do you want from me?" I said aloud, but only silence followed. Without thinking, I punched the tree and blood oozed from my knuckles.

Jonah stopped beside me. He bent over, hands on his knees, catching his breath. When he noticed my bloody knuckles, he took off his jacket and wrapped it around my hand, then sat cross-legged next to me. "Hey. It's OK."

"No it's not!"

"What did your dad tell you? Talk to me."

"Why do you want to know? So you can pray for me? Or so you can tell me this was God's will? I'm sick of hearing about your God and how good He is!" Breathing hard, my teeth clenched, I pummeled Jonah with my fists until he grabbed my wrists and held them.

"I know you're upset, but listen to me."

Struggling to free myself, I finally realized he was stronger than I was, so I went limp and leaned against him, fitting easily into his arms as if I were the last piece in a jigsaw puzzle.

"Bad things happen, but God doesn't make them happen. We make our own choices, and so do the people around us."

"But God doesn't stop the bad things."

Jonah shook his head slowly. "The Bible says God works all things together for good for those who love Him."

Love Him? I didn't love Him! "Shut up! Just shut up! My mother rolled her car. She could have been killed. And my sister died, Jonah. She was five years old. Where's the good in that? How do you expect me to trust a God who lets stuff like this happen?"

"I know how you feel, but—"

"You don't know! My mother drinks too much. That's probably why she crashed the car. And you've never been responsible for somebody's death."

Jonah let out a long sigh. "In a way, I was." He pulled his knees to his chest and bowed his head as if he couldn't look me in the face to explain.

Bam. Just like that, he had my attention. I thought I'd misunderstood what he'd said, but I was pretty sure I hadn't. I waited, wondering how I'd missed this about Jonah. He always seemed so together. I thought he had life figured out, and well, if he didn't have all the answers, he could talk to somebody who did— God.

"Three years ago," he said, "I was hanging out with some older guys who thought fun meant getting high. We stole prescription drugs from our parents' medicine cabinets, then we'd throw them into a bowl, mix them up and down a handful. You never knew what you were taking, or what the combination would do to you. It was Russian roulette. What you knew for sure though was you'd check out of your life for a while, maybe permanently. I was only thirteen."

I stared at Jonah open-mouthed. Him? Saint Jonah? The Jesus Kid? No way.

He lifted his head and stared into my eyes. "Surprised? We're all sinners, but a lot of us won't admit it, and we won't ask for forgiveness."

I never would have guessed this about Jonah. He didn't fit into the picture he'd just painted inside my head. "So what happened three years ago?"

"Did you notice the handicap ramp at my house?"

I didn't have the nerve to ask him about it. I figured if he wanted to tell me, he would. Nodding, I kept quiet, sensing this was hard for him to talk about.

"Me and my so-called friends were partying one night. It got late. My parents were worried, and Dad called my cell. I was more wasted than usual. We were at Will's—his parents were out of town—and like an idiot, I'd climbed out an upstairs window and sat on the roof of a two-story house, feeling like I could fly. My dad told me not to move, that he'd come and get me..." Jonah's voice grew softer with every word.

I could see through him now, how vulnerable he was, how much pain this had caused him. My first instinct was to bombard him with questions, but sometimes the best thing you could do for a friend was just listen, so I reached over and took his hand in mine. For a few minutes, neither of us spoke.

"It was a Saturday night," he went on. "Two in the morning. My dad pounded on Will's door, and finally the guys let him inside. He slipped through the same window I'd gone out. He was on his way to rescue me when he fell."

For the first time since I'd met Jonah, he was relying on me, instead of the other way around. "Go ahead. You can tell me everything."

Jonah gave me a weak smile, then rested his forehead against one hand and shook his head. "Somebody called 911, I don't even remember who, and an ambulance took my dad away. The next time I saw him, he was in a hospital bed, hooked up to tubes and wires in the ICU." Jonah covered his eyes with his hands. "My dad's in a wheelchair because of me."

Worry flickered in his eyes, as if he expected me to hate him after his confession. "He didn't die in the accident, but everything changed for him. His old life definitely ended."

Wow. "I'm sorry. How did you get over it?"

He shook his head. "You never get over it. You just learn to live with the guilt."

"How?" If Jonah had done it, maybe I could too.

"My mother pretty much forced me to go to a week long summer camp out in the middle of nowhere. A Bible camp. On the last night, we were sitting around a campfire and the group leader handed out little strips of paper and told us to write down anything we were struggling with in our lives. I wrote 'drugs' and 'my dad's accident.' Then the guy said if we wanted to, we could give those problems to God, and so we threw our papers into the fire and watched them burn. Something changed for me that night. I knew I needed God in my life."

It sounded simple. Admit your mistakes. Ask for forgiveness. Just let go of your problems. "But you said the guilt never goes away. So what changed?"

"Me. My attitude. I started going to church with my family again. I joined the youth group, and I made new friends. I don't need to get high anymore to feel good." Jonah stood and offered me his hand. "Come on. We'd better get back."

Side by side, we walked across the parking lot holding hands, and Jonah held the door open for me. In the waiting room, my dad still sat in the same corner of the room, sipping his coffee, and we claimed the chairs beside him. I tried to focus on what Jonah had told me, how he'd changed, how maybe with his help and Candra's help, I could change too.

But terrible thoughts kept invading my brain. Mom was drunk. What if she couldn't quit drinking, and she wasn't so lucky next time?

26

A half hour later, a bubbly, the-glass-is-half-full nurse approached us. "Mr. Werthman?" You can go see your wife now. This way."

Jonah gave me a quick hug. "I'll be here when you come back."

Following the nurse through the doors—where no one was allowed without permission—and down a white-tiled hallway, shiny as ice glinting in the neon-bathed light, I tried not to think about my sister, but everything I saw here reminded me of the day of the accident. The day my little sister was brought to a hospital emergency room, but we never took her home. *This is different. Mom's OK. Lacerations. A bump on the head. She will go home.*

Mom's eyes were closed when we stepped into the room, but they fluttered open as soon as we moved beside her bed. A thermal blanket was pulled up to her chin. Tiny bits of glass clung to her scalp, adhered with dried blood. There was a huge black and blue mark in the center of her forehead. Cuts and bruises covered both arms.

She looked from Dad to me, and her eyes filled with tears. "I'm so sorry."

Dad took her hand, and she didn't yank it out of his grasp. Watching Mom's face, he leaned over—probably on guard in case she told him to stop—and kissed her forehead. "I'm just glad you're all right."

This was the closest I'd seen them act in months. In fact, no matter how they'd been treating each other, today, it was easy to see they still cared. I waited for Dad to ask her whether she'd been drinking, but he never did. Didn't he want to know?

Mom squeezed his hand. When she blinked, it forced the tears to slide down her cheeks. Her face looked blotchy, so she'd obviously been crying before we came.

"No, listen," Mom said. "I shouldn't have been driving."

"Shhh. It'll be all right," Dad said.

Dad should have been furious with her, but he didn't seem mad at all.

Mom swiped the tears away with the back of her hand. "The police were here."

"What did they say?" he asked gently.

Mom shook her head. "Apparently some guy spotted my car in the ditch. I guess I'd been there for several hours before anybody noticed. I told the police I didn't remember what happened. And it's the truth." She grabbed the side rail of the bed and pulled herself up straighter, wincing as if she were in pain. "Where are my clothes? I want to go home."

"You have to wait," Dad said. "The doctor has to sign your release."

She settled back against the thin mattress. "I just want to go home and forget about this horrible day."

"Were you drinking?" I asked. My words cut through her. She looked wounded, scared. It was strange, seeing my mother like this, so vulnerable, because even when she was drunk, she still seemed in control.

"Lauren!" Dad said. "Not now."

I sank into the chair pushed against the wall at the foot of the bed, sorry I'd upset my dad, but not sorry for what I'd said to Mom.

"When this is over," Mom said in a shaky voice, "I promise you guys, things are going to be different. I'll get help. I'll do whatever it takes."

Jonah thought everything happened for a reason, because God had a plan for our lives. Maybe something like this needed to happen so she'd finally see her drinking was out of control.

The same nurse entered the room. Dad moved aside, and I started to get up out of my chair, but the nurse said, "No, you guys are fine." She wrapped a blood pressure cuff around Mom's arm, pumped the bulb until the cuff tightened, and released with a whoosh of air. "Still a little high," she said, writing numbers on a chart. She smiled, which seemed ridiculous to me. What was there to smile about? Didn't she realize my mother could have killed herself or somebody else?

"How are you feeling, Mrs. Werthman?" the nurse asked. "Any dizziness? How's your pain on a scale of one to ten, ten being the worst pain you can imagine?"

"It's not bad," Mom mumbled. "Two, I guess." She turned toward the windows.

"Anything I can get you? Would you like something to eat?"

Mom's bottom lip trembled. "No, thank you. I'm not hungry. How soon can I leave?"

"We want to keep you overnight for observation. You took a pretty hard blow to the head."

Rolling over onto her back, Mom's eyes held a desperate look. "My family can keep an eye on me tonight."

"The doctor recommended you spend the night here," the nurse said in a soothing tone. "We're trying to find you a room. It shouldn't take much longer. And then if everything looks good tomorrow, I'm sure he'll release you." She slipped out of the room before Mom could protest.

I'm not sure why I said what I said next. Maybe it was because Mom looked so pathetic, or maybe it was because I knew how it felt to make a really big mistake. For whatever reason, I said, "I could stay with you."

Mom's eyes widened and her lips parted slightly, as if I'd said the most shocking thing she'd heard for a long time.

"Honey," Dad said, "you have school tomorrow, remember? But it was sweet of you to offer. I'll stay."

Mom shook her head. "You can both go home. I'm fine."

"No, somebody should stick around," Dad said. "The nurses are so busy. It can take them forever to come after you push the call button."

"You could call school in the morning," I said, "and tell them I'm not coming." Shut up! What was wrong with me? I guess in some perverted way, I was enjoying the fact that Mom was miserable, not me, and this was her mistake not mine. But all night, cooped up in a hospital room, just her and I? We'd have to talk, wouldn't we? And what would we talk about?

"OK, then it's settled. If you don't mind staying, Lauren, I can run your friend Jonah home."

"The boy who came to our house?" Mom said. "The religious one? What's he doing here? Please tell me he doesn't know all the details."

And there was the mother I knew, the woman who feared other people's opinions, who was all about projecting a positive image even if it was fake.

"He was worried about me," I said.

Mom's jaw clenched and all remorse vanished from her expression. "Well, I don't want you sharing our private business."

When Haley died, we had no privacy. Reporters and cameramen stalked us for weeks. We couldn't pull out of our driveway or walk to the mailbox without some idiot trying to shove a microphone in front of our faces. Dad called them vultures who fed off of other people's misery.

"I promise you guys, things are going to be different." Sure, Mom, whatever. They were just words she thought we wanted to hear. She wasn't sorry.

"Why don't you go out and see if your friend's ready to leave?" Dad asked. "I'll keep your mom company."

In the waiting room, Jonah sat near the TV, flipping through the pages of a magazine. He glanced up as I walked toward him, then he stood and opened his arms and I slid into them, a shelter from everything wrong in the world. When I was with Jonah, when he was holding me, I didn't have to think about Haley, or my mother, or gym class. Inside his arms I felt safe.

"How's she doing?" he asked.

"She's...shaken up. More worried than I've ever seen her before."

"How are you doing?"

"I'm scared for her. For my family. I'm spending the night here. My dad wanted me to ask you if you're ready to go yet. He can give you a ride home."

"Yeah, but do you mind if I pray for your family before I leave? I think there's a chapel here." Jonah kissed the top of my head.

Well, what harm could it do? "I thought you could pray anywhere."

"You can, but I want to feel as close to God as possible, you know?"

"I guess." Maybe it was easier to think of the right words to say if you were in a church. "Can I come with you?" Where had that come from? I hadn't been inside a church since I was small, since I'd stopped believing anybody heard the prayers I said.

"Sure."

After letting my dad know where we were going, Jonah and I rode the elevator to the sixth floor, where Miss Cheerful, Mom's nurse, had told us we'd find the chapel. Stained glass window panels glowed in the front of the room, and a table held a carved, wooden cross where a man hung—Jesus. Candles flickered in votive cups. Nobody else was there, which was good, because I felt like a fraud. I didn't believe in the God Jonah believed in, and I was sure if anyone else saw me, they'd know I was an imposter just by looking at me.

"Come on," Jonah said, striding to the first row. He slid onto the pew, folded his hands, and bowed his head.

I squeezed next to him and did exactly the same thing. My dad told me once, "If you want to be happy, act like you're happy." I wanted to believe there was a God, Somebody who truly cared about us, so, following the same logic, I figured I'd pretend there was One.

Jonah took my hand in his, and I didn't feel so alone. It was as if he shared this problem with me. "Dear God," Jonah said, "Thank you for all you've done for me. Thank you for all you've done for Lauren and her family."

What had God done for me and my family? Nothing good. Nothing worth thanking him for.

"Lord, You know what's happening now, and You're still in control. Please bless Lauren's mom. Heal her. Heal this family. Give the doctors and nurses the knowledge they need to care for her mom's injuries. All things are possible with You, Lord. And, God, give Lauren the courage to invite You into her life. She needs You. We ask this in Jesus's name. Amen."

As I sat there next to Jonah, holding tight to his hand, and, in spite of all that had happened, a calmness swept over me.

I wanted what Jonah had. Not a perfect life. Not a no problems kind of life, but a life where Somebody was looking out for me, Somebody who could point me in the right direction when I strayed too far and got lost and forgot where I was supposed to go. Did my life have a purpose?

"I need help," I whispered. And I think Jonah knew I wasn't talking to him.

27

Mom drifted in and out of sleep. Doctors strode by, silver stethoscopes dangling from their necks, white jackets flapping in the self-created breeze. Nurses padded past the doorway, wearing quiet-as-cat-paws shoes. Announcements floated from the P.A. system, requesting doctors to report to the O.R., stat.

Rolling over in the narrow bed, Mom moaned, and I touched her arm, figuring she was having a bad dream about the car accident.

Her eyes flew open and she looked disoriented for a moment, but then she gazed at me. "You didn't need to stay."

Typical. She didn't want my help. She didn't appreciate it.

Her gaze swiveled toward the clock on the wall. Then she swallowed and reached out with a shaky hand for the pitcher of water sitting on the bedside table, almost knocking it over.

I jumped up. "I'll get it."

"No, I've got it," she insisted, fingers closing around the handle. As she lifted the pitcher it tipped sideways and water splashed from the spout, slopping onto her lap. "Darn it!"

Yanking a handful of paper towels from the dispenser, I handed them to her. "I could have helped you."

She dabbed at the sheet, trying to blot up the spill.

"I just want to be alone."

I hardly knew her anymore. Grief did things to you. It changed you, turned you into somebody who stumbled through the motions of living, but every positive feeling you ever had withered and died.

I wanted my mother back. "That's all you ever want to do. Be alone."

"Did you stay so you could say disrespectful things to me? I am still your mother."

No, she hadn't been my mother since Haley died. I'd lost both of them. "You don't act like it," I mumbled, wishing I could take it back the second I'd said it. I was such an idiot.

The color drained from her face. "What did you say? Hand me the phone."

She wanted to call Dad to come and get me. Even though I wanted to leave, we needed to have this conversation.

"Did you hear me?" Her voice rumbled to life, a thunderstorm gathering more force. "Hand me the phone!"

I crossed my arms, but didn't move. "So you can send me away?"

"What is the matter with you?" She hit the button on the bed, and it slowly groaned to a more upright position, one where she could lock eyes with me, pin me with her glare. "I was just in a car accident and you're standing there giving me backtalk."

I had no words of comfort to offer, because every time I looked at her, I thought of what might have happened. Mom was so selfish to get in the car and drive in her condition. It never occurred to her she might harm somebody else.

And it never occurred to you Haley could get hurt

while you yakked on your cellphone that day. You didn't bother to check on her. My heart beat furiously, like an insect beating its wings against the sides of a glass jar. A jar with no air holes.

Pacing the room, I was trapped by one ugly truth and my words tumbled out in an avalanche of emotion: "You're just sorry I'm the one who's still here."

She looked as if I'd struck her. "What a terrible thing to say to me."

Throwing my hands in the air, I stomped to the side of her bed. "I screwed up! I'm sorry! Are you going to blame me for the rest of my life?"

Tears filled her eyes. "No...I don't know. I look at you and I think about Haley and how I'll never see her again."

Then it hit me. I knew why Mom couldn't stand me, because I felt the same way about her right then. She should have known better than to drink and drive. I should have known better than to ignore my sister. If I had looked in on her, then maybe she wouldn't have drowned.

The nurse bolted through the doorway. "Everything OK in here?" she asked, the toothpaste-ad-worthy smile missing from her face. The corners of her mouth went slack as she looked from Mom to me. "Good news," she said, with a let's-change-the-subject smile.

I suspected even when she had bad news, she put her own positive spin on it. Great news! Your husband needs a triple bypass, but there's a fifty percent chance he'll survive! Isn't that wonderful?

"We have a room ready for your mom," the nurse said. "You can meet us upstairs. Room 615."

Stay tuned, I thought. Round two, the sixth floor. Where the chapel was. Fate or divine intervention? I knew how Jonah would vote.

"See you there," I said.

Minutes later, the elevator droned in a mechanical voice, "Sixth floor." I stepped out and a bell sounded as the stainless steel doors sealed shut behind me. No turning back. I was there, and I was going to stay. Mom and I had to talk this out or neither one of us would ever get past it.

Except for two nurses, the hallway—with its blue commercial carpeting and peaceful landscape paintings—was deserted. Over-sized potted plants stretched leafy fingers toward the sunlight filtered through the blinds on the window next to the elevators.

Traveling down the hall, I watched the room numbers grow larger—601, 602, 603—and I kept walking until I rounded the corner and started up the other side clear to the end. Hesitating outside 615, I glanced at the room opposite Mom's and saw the engraved gold plate on the wall: Chapel.

No way. Mom's room was right across from the chapel? I pushed through the door of room 615. There were two beds, both unoccupied. Maybe Mom would get a roommate, and then we couldn't talk. Nobody talked about serious stuff in front of a stranger. We could pretend we were a normal mother and daughter, people who felt comfortable with each other, who were perfectly OK with watching TV together in silence.

I crossed the room, looked down from the double window and had a bird's eye view of the parking lot with its rows of cars. From here, they seemed the size of toys. People bustled to and from the front entrance.

Trees cast multi-fingered shadows on the plush green grass.

"Hi," a singsong voice said. The nurse was blonde, petite and definitely perky. She and another nurse pushed my mom's gurney into the room and parked it parallel to the bed. "On my count," the perky nurse said. "One, two, three." Together they lifted Mom onto the mattress, and the other nurse padded out of the room.

"I'm Hope," the blonde said. "I'll be your mom's nurse today."

Hope. I looked up and wondered if there was something to this God business, and if He was directing tonight's events. Maybe Jonah's prayers had gotten through to Somebody after all.

"And you are...?" Hope asked.

"The daughter."

"Does the daughter have a name?" Hope grinned.

"Lauren."

"Well, Lauren, let me know if you or your mom need anything. The cafeteria's open till nine, or we can have some food sent to the room and you can eat together. The TV remote's right here," she said pointing, "and I'll clip the call button to the bed next to Mom, OK?"

"Thanks."

Hope stepped toward the door. "Be back soon," she called over her shoulder.

Mom turned away from me, facing the window. It was going to be a long night.

I grabbed the remote and flicked through the channels, finally settling on a soap opera where every actor had bigger problems than any human being could possibly encounter in one lifetime. Pushing the chair over in front of the window, I sank into the seat and stared blankly at the screen, grateful for the distraction.

After a few minutes, Mom turned toward me and said, "Why'd you really volunteer to stay?"

Good question. I wasn't sure myself. I just felt like I needed to stay. "I miss you," I finally whispered, surprised by my own answer.

Silence. Had I said the wrong thing again?

"What's the name of your school psychologist?" she asked.

She was going to lecture me about going to therapy, make sure I'd signed up for a life-long membership to the crazy-of-the-month club. "Candra. Miss Gladden."

"When do you see her again?"

"She's been out of town, but she'll be back on Monday."

"Would it be all right with you if we talked to her together?"

What? My mother didn't believe in talking about her problems. Oh, sure it was fine if I peeled open my heart, removed the protective covering like the skin on an orange, until the delicate inner layers were exposed. But not Mom. She never let people see how she truly felt. "I guess so."

For the first time since Haley's death, my mother had offered to support me.

28

Monday morning, clouds hovered over a steel-gray sky. For the entire first period, I worried what Mom would think of Candra. My mother wasn't the most open-minded person. She'd zero in on Candra's multiple piercings, her cornrows, her unconventional clothes, and she'd come to the conclusion this wasn't somebody who should help a kid deal with their problems, let alone somebody who should work for the public school system. But she'd offered to come and talk to Candra. With me. That was huge.

By the time the bell rang, I'd chewed my fingernails down to nothing. I shot out of my seat, wishing I could inhale a half-gallon of cookie dough ice cream smothered in chocolate syrup. "When you crave food," Candra had told me, "pay attention to how you're feeling. Usually an emotion is behind the craving."

Well, she was right. My emotions were all over the place, little silver balls in a pinball machine, pinging against my nerves. I hadn't dreaded going to Candra's office since the first day Mr. Bixby sent me there, but throw Mom into the equation, and visiting Candra had pitched me into a full blown anxiety attack.

When I reached her office, Mom wasn't there yet, thank God. Just Harley, racing around his wheel, and Candra, wearing a long, crinkly skirt, and a peasant blouse with puffy sleeves.

"Hey!" Candra said, looking up from studying the papers blanketing the top of her desk. Her dangly, multi-colored earrings hung like mini-chandeliers and reflected the fluorescent lights. She smiled, scooped the papers in a pile, and then fed them to a file folder before propping her boots on her desk. "Tell me what I missed while I was gone. Besides you."

I shrugged. "Oh, you know, just the usual. Tiffany passed out in the girls' bathroom, and a few days ago, my mother landed in the hospital."

Candra's eyes bugged out under lashes coated with thick black mascara and lids painted a deep blue. "Wait. Back up the bus. Explain, please."

"Miss Gladden?" Mom strode in, wearing low-heeled shoes, cream-colored slacks, and a matching blazer. I watched for her pleasant expression to crash as she took inventory of Candra, but it never happened.

Candra swung her legs from her desk as if someone had yelled at her to get her feet off the furniture. She rose and offered Mom her hand. "You must be Lauren's mom. So good to meet you."

"Likewise," Mom said, shaking her hand. "Lauren speaks very highly of you."

"I kind of like her too." Candra winked at me. "She told me you were coming today. Have a seat. What can I do for you?"

Mom lowered herself into a chair, folded her hands in her lap, and picked at her fingernails, something she did when she was nervous. I didn't think she was going to say anything, but then, her eyes cast down, she said, "I know Lauren's been seeing you for a while now. How's she doing?"

So. Mom hadn't come to talk about herself. This

was about me—the broken kid no therapist had been able to fix yet. The daughter with terrible eating habits. The one who'd gained so much weight, my mother was probably ashamed for people to see us together.

"Lauren's made real progress, but as you know, healing from a traumatic experience takes time."

Mom wouldn't know about that. She wasn't trying to heal. She'd dived into the deep end of depression, and she was holding her breath, refusing to come up for air.

"So she told you about Haley?" Mom asked. For an instant, her eyes held a light, twin candles of hope, but then the light flickered as if drowning in pools of wax.

Candra glanced at me, cleared her throat. "Her sister? No, not really. I know something happened to her. And Mr. Bixby, our principal, requested Lauren come here instead of going to gym class, but that's about the extent of my knowledge."

Mom looked at me and I read the question in her eyes: "Do you want to tell her, or should I? It's time."

Closing my eyes, I pictured a mound of greasy French fries and a thick hamburger smothered with pickles, ketchup, and onions. I could almost taste the salty fries and hot onions, could almost see the steam rising from the juicy burger, just waiting for me to sink my teeth into it. *Stop it. You're just like Mom.* Except she used alcohol to stop the hurt, not food.

When it came right down to it, Mom and I were not much different.

"My youngest daughter, Haley," Mom whispered, "died about two months ago."

"I'm so sorry," Candra said. "It must be very difficult for you and your whole family."

She understood—we were still struggling. It wasn't something we were supposed to have gotten over by this time.

"Yes," Mom muttered. "I'm afraid I haven't done a very good job of dealing with it."

Neither have I.

"Well, you came here today. That tells me you want to begin healing." Candra opened a desk drawer. "I can refer you to some excellent family therapists."

"No," Mom said simply. "You're the first counselor Lauren's talked to that she's liked. I want her to continue coming here, and I don't want to see someone else either."

Candra held eye contact with Mom for several seconds before she spoke. "OK. Lauren, are you ready to tell me about Haley? Have you talked about what happened to her with your Mom?"

Trapped again. I was the firefly in the glass jar. Pounding, beating against the enclosure, desperate for a way out. "I don't think I can."

Mom touched my arm, her lips curving into a quivering smile. "It's OK. We need to talk about this. Just tell her what happened."

I swallowed. Talking about it would hurt Mom for sure. And what would Candra think of me after she knew? But they'd herded me into a corner and I had no escape. "I was in my room with the door closed, talking to my best friend on my cell. Haley barged in like three times, whining and wanting me to play with her."

"So you were babysitting?"

"Yeah. During the summer, I watched her every day while my parents worked."

"Big responsibility," Candra said, folding her

hands in her lap. "How'd you feel about that?"

"I didn't like it. I wanted to go do stuff with my friends."

"Did your parents pay you for watching Haley?"

"No."

"Did you resent your parents for making you babysit?"

Mom didn't flinch. She didn't interrupt. It was as if she was hanging on my every word.

"I guess so." Haley was an obstacle in the way of me enjoying my summer vacation. I'd wished a million times I didn't have a younger sister.

"So basically, you're saying Haley behaved like a bratty little sister?"

I stole a glance at Mom, expecting to see anger in her eyes, because Candra had just insulted her precious child, and everybody knew you weren't supposed to say bad things about the dead, but Mom just leaned forward in her chair, waiting for my answer.

"Well, yeah," I said. "I told her to get out of my room. And she did. For a while. But then she came back, wearing her swimsuit, and she said unless I took her swimming, right away, she was going to tell Mom how mean I'd been to her."

"So Haley wanted you to walk to the pool with her?" Candra asked.

"No," Mom said, tears welling in her eyes. "In Minnesota, we had an in-ground pool. It had a fence around it, but somehow Haley got inside."

"Lauren, go on," Candra said. "Haley came back, and then what happened?"

In my mind, I saw my sister, standing in my doorway, wearing her pink flip-flops, her cartoon character swimsuit, and plastic sunglasses. "Get off the phone!" she'd hollered, stomping her foot. "You promised you'd go to the pool with me."

My throat seized up like when you have strep throat and you can't swallow because it hurts so bad. My tongue wouldn't cooperate with my mouth to form words.

"Honey, it's OK," Mom said so gently it almost made me cry. "Tell us what happened next."

Mom had never asked to hear all the details. Our eyes met. I wasn't sure she was ready for what I was about to say. "I told her she could wait until you guys got home from work. She kicked my door and had a meltdown, saying she was going to tell on me, but she finally left. I didn't hear her again. When I finished talking on the phone, I turned on my laptop and scrolled through Facebook. I didn't go check on Haley. I should have checked on her."

Candra waited, silently urging me to go on, but I couldn't. I couldn't tell her the ending to this sad story. Mom picked at her nails, wiped a stray tear from her face, but she said nothing.

"She drowned?" Candra asked quietly.

"Yeah," I said. "Mom came home from work and asked me where Haley was, and I told her she was in her room. The next thing I heard was Mom screaming, like someone was stabbing her. I ran to the backyard, and Mom was kneeling beside my sister, doing CPR." I swallowed through the dull ache in my throat. "But it was too late."

By this time, both Mom and I were clutching each other's hands so hard our knuckles had turned white.

Candra nodded and listened. She pushed a tissue box toward us, leaving it up to us whether or not we needed one. Then Candra said, "Mom, have you ever told Lauren this was an accident? That it wasn't her fault?"

My mother shook her head. "It wasn't Lauren's fault," she said, her breath hitching on tears. "I took a swim the night before. I must have forgotten to lock the gate."

29

For the rest of the morning, I wandered from class to class, lost in a fog of thought. "I must have forgotten to lock the gate," Mom had said. All this time, I believed she blamed me for Haley's death, but her own guilt had been gnawing away at her heart. It must have been so hard to admit what she'd done.

My steps felt a little lighter as I crossed the long hallway leading to the cafeteria. Yes, I should have paid more attention to Haley the day of the accident, but just knowing it hadn't been entirely my fault, had given me something to look forward to: a new life. One I might even deserve.

I found Jonah slouched at our usual table, listening to his iPod, his tray already loaded with food. I flung my book bag on the floor next to his feet and dropped onto the bench.

"Hey!" His arm twined around me. "How did the meeting go with Miss Gladden and your mom? Jazz waited for you, but she had to stop by the music room."

I'd told him last night about Mom coming to school to talk to Miss Gladden, and he knew we weren't getting along, but he didn't know why. What was I supposed to say? I'm only half responsible for my sister's death? Did that make me any less guilty?

"Lauren? Do you want to talk about it?"

"Not here."

He leaned in, his forehead touching mine, his hair brushing against my face. "Are you OK?" he whispered.

"No, but I'm better."

"Aren't you going to get something to eat?" he asked.

"I'm not hungry." And I wasn't. Nothing sounded good. Not even ice cream.

Jonah stood and grabbed his tray. "You know what? Neither am I." He carried the tray over to a trash can, scraped the food off his plate, then set everything on the conveyor belt and it disappeared into the kitchen. "C'mon. Let's take a walk." He held out his hand, and I took it, grateful for his company. Together we strolled out of the cafeteria.

The pavement was wet from the morning rain, and we stepped around puddles and dodged earthworms who'd abandoned the soggy soil. We walked to the stone benches surrounding the flagpole. Except for a few kids leaning against the building, there was no one else close by.

"You know you can tell me anything," Jonah said, "and I'll still be here for you." He smiled. "Just like God."

I leaned my head against his chest and he held me for the longest time, his heartbeat a steady throb in my ear.

"You know I had a sister," I said, looking up at him. "Haley. She drowned in our swimming pool when she was five years old." I hesitated, not wanting to confess everything. "I...was babysitting her the day she died."

Jonah hugged me tighter and kissed the top of my head. "Wow," he finally said. "What an awful secret to keep to yourself."

"It's why I freaked out the first day of school."

"When you saw the swimming pool."

"Yeah. Do you think I'm a terrible person?" I could tell by how soft his voice had been, and how he still had his arms around me that he didn't think I was at all, but I needed to hear him say it.

"No. I think you're a girl who had something terrible happen to her. You know what else I think?"

I shook my head, and he leaned in close, our faces inches apart, his breath warm and soft against my forehead. His kiss was gentle but then grew possessive, as if he was claiming me, like he wanted me to belong to him. "I think I love you," he whispered.

He loved me? Did he really just say that?

Feet scuffled and something hit the cement.

We turned toward the sound, and just as Eli reached for the runaway bottle of water, our eyes met.

He looked as if he'd just lost the only friend he had in the entire world, and then his stare turned dull, and he seemed to look right through me. He snatched the bottle and fumbled to hold onto his sketchpad, but it slipped from beneath his arm and landed with a splat in standing rainwater. "Crud!" he said, pulling it toward him, the pages dripping wet.

"Eli!" I called. "Wait up."

Without any acknowledgement, he turned away from me and shuffled through the door.

When you've been there, it's easy to spot hopelessness on somebody else's face. Was it my fault? Did he think we were more than just friends? He'd probably seen the kiss. "I have to find him, Jonah."

"Do you want me to come with you?"

"No. I think I should talk to him alone."

I stood on tiptoes and kissed Jonah goodbye. "I love you too. See you later."

Zigzagging around kids in the hallway, I searched for a set of spindly legs, ratty shoes with holey air-conditioning, and somebody carrying a sketchpad under one arm. Where would Eli go? Someplace he could be alone. Someplace he could escape the pain. Escape the pain. He wouldn't try to hurt himself, would he? Please God, keep Eli safe. Show me where he is.

"Did you see Eli Fleming in there?" I asked a guy exiting the boys' bathroom.

He shook his hair back so it feathered against his forehead, an I'm-a-cool-jock move. Then looking me over from head to toe, probably weighing how it would affect his popularity if he spoke to me, he graced me with three words: "That freak? Nah."

Why was everyone so mean to Eli? He hadn't done anything to them. But he was different, looked geeky, and that was enough to make him a target, someone they enjoyed shooting insults at. I could have been nicer too, instead of trying to get rid of him every time he came around.

"He's not a freak!" I said louder than I'd intended, causing kids to rubberneck and giggle.

"OK," the guy said, raising his hands. "Whatever you say, L.B." Swaggering away, I heard him and the guy walking next to him crack up at my expense.

Great. Tiffany's nickname for me had spread like an epidemic. Well, it didn't matter. I had to find Eli. *Try the art room. Where you first met him.* I hurried down the next corridor, hung a right at the end of the hallway and pushed through the door. The lights were off. Easels stood in a circular pattern like a sleeping herd, supporting canvases with half-finished paintings.

Way in the back of the room, I noticed legs and feet behind an easel. A sketchpad was lying on the floor. "Eli? Is that you?"

Moving slowly, I crossed the room until I could see his greasy hair hanging down, shadowing his zit-filled forehead, his knobby knees poking out under tattered jeans, and his tie-dyed tee-shirt, the colors dulled from too many washings. One white sock had lost its elastic top and pooled around his skinny ankle. He was bent at the waist. Doing what? Thinking? Crying? I couldn't tell.

"L-L-Leave me alone!" he shouted.

What had I done? "Are you all right?"

"L-L-Like you care."

Inching forward, I walked in a wide arc until I was standing to his side about twelve feet away. The fingers of his right hand grasped something, and those fingers rested on top of his left wrist.

"I do care," I said, trying to get a better look. "You're my friend."

Raising his head, his eyes glistened. He seemed to see me, but the far away hopeless look was still there. "I...thought you understood. I thought we were the same."

He drew his fingers across his wrist and a bright red line appeared. Blood. He must be holding a razor blade. Oh, no. He'd cut himself. But the line remained thin. Not a deep wound. Not life threatening.

"Don't," I said.

"W-W-Why not?" He smiled the kind of smile you managed when you knew your situation would never improve. "Nobody cares what happens to me." His fingers hovered over his wrist again.

"I do." *Stop it. Don't do it again.*

"No you don't. Not really. I heard you. You love Jonah." Another angry red line appeared on his wrist, deeper than the first. Blood dripped down his arm now.

What should I do? Was he trying to kill himself, or just punish me by making me watch this self-mutilation? "Eli, please stop."

"Why? Does it bother you?"

I didn't miss the sarcasm and defiance in his voice. Definitely trying to punish me. I'd never led him on. Maybe he misread me because not many kids were nice to him. "Yes it bothers me! Look, Eli. I know how you feel."

"You don't have a clue!"

Drops of blood hit the floor. I glanced in all directions, searching for something to hold against his arm to stop the bleeding. My gaze landed on the sink behind Eli and the paper towel dispenser hanging on the wall.

"Calm down. Let's talk, OK?"

"F-F-Fine. You...don't get it, do you? Kids like us, we have to stick together. Otherwise girls like Tiffany...they win. They just keep at you until you can't take it anymore, you know?"

God, please give me the right words to say. "Yeah, I know. Right now, you've had it with everything. You feel like giving up, right?"

Surprise flickered across his face and some of his anger drained away. He nodded.

Keep talking to him. It's working. I took a few cautious steps. I had to stop the bleeding. "I've been seeing Miss Gladden. She can help you too."

"How? Look at me. I'm a geek." He studied his

arm, the two lines of blood, the drops on the white tile floor. Glancing up at me he said, "W-W-Why'd you need to see her, anyway?"

I had to tell him. Honesty was the only way he'd believe a word I said. "My little sister died because of me. She drowned. If I can live with that, you can live with bullying."

He pursed his thin lips as if considering this. "B-B-But I don't have any friends."

"You have me. And Jonah and Jazz will be your friends too."

"I'm...sorry about your sister." He stood and pushed the stool back, pivoting toward the sink. Turning the faucet on, he stuck his arm under the running water. The blood swirled down the drain. After a few seconds, he turned the faucet off.

"Thank you." Relief settled over me like a quilt on a cold night. I moved forward until I was standing next to him and yanked out a handful of paper towels, pressing them against his wrist. "We need to go to the nurse."

"N-N-No! She can't find out what I did."

"What if it doesn't stop bleeding?"

"It will. I've done this before."

"OK. I won't tell on one condition. You have to go to Miss Gladden's office. Right now."

He looked panicky, his eyes darting from me to the door. "S-S-She'll call my mom."

"Maybe not. Were you trying to kill yourself?"

He shook his head. "The cutting, it helps me deal with the bad stuff, you know?"

I nodded. "I eat. A lot. That's how I deal. It'll be OK. Just tell Miss Gladden the truth. You can't keep doing this, Eli." Lifting the paper towels, I checked his arm. It took a few seconds for the cuts to turn red again. The flow had slowed down. Finally. I pressed down harder on his arm.

"Let go," he said, holding the towels in place himself.

I stooped to pick up his sketchpad. Water dripped from the pages.

"I-I-It's ruined," he said.

Smiling, I tucked it under my arm. "Don't worry. You can start over."

"Y-Y-Yeah." He offered his own gap-toothed smile.

As soon as his arm quit bleeding, I'd walk him to Miss Gladden's office, no excuses, no detours.

"You…know something, Lauren?"

"What?"

"Y-Y-You are different."

"Different bad or different good?"

I saw the whole top row of his yellowed teeth when he smiled broader. "G-G-Good. Definitely good."

30

Courtney—the girl whose face I'd smacked with a soccer ball—glided into history class the next day wearing a skin-tight tee-shirt and jeans that clung so tight they must have been cutting off the circulation to her legs.

I scooted lower in my seat, expecting her to shoot me a crusty look, but when she did glance my way, her expression was neutral. She ditched her book bag under her desk, and then turned and strolled toward me.

I could tell by the way chairs swiveled around the other kids anticipated a scene. Just what I needed. At least Tiffany wasn't there yet, so the two of them couldn't gang up on me.

Courtney stopped next to my desk, one hand propped on her hip. You had to look closely to notice the three tiny stitches below her bottom lip. Although her mouth was still slightly swollen and a little black-and-blue, her face didn't look Frankenstein-ish at all.

"Hey," Courtney said to me. "I just wanted you to know I'm not mad about the whole stitches thing. I get them out in a couple days. It was an accident, so don't sweat it, OK?"

Stunned, I couldn't think of anything to say for a moment. "Well…thanks."

Her lip-glossed mouth curved into a smile. "No

problem. Oh, and congrats on making the team. You're a great goalie."

No way. "I made the soccer team?"

"You didn't know? Miss Torrens posted the list outside the gym door this morning."

Tiffany sauntered in, noticed us talking and rushed over. "Courtney! You're back!" They both threw their arms around each other and swayed back and forth hugging.

When they separated, Courtney held a hand in front of her mouth like she was embarrassed.

Tiffany reached up and pulled her hand away. "Let me see. Oh, they aren't so bad."

"Just a couple more days," Courtney said, "and they'll be gone. The doctor said there shouldn't be a scar."

"I'm glad," I said. Both girls eyed me, and I wished I hadn't said anything. I waited for Tiffany to attack me, waited for her to give me the speech: "You owe her. You have to pay for what you did."

But Mr. Hazzard interrupted. "Good morning, people." He swaggered up to the front of the room. "If you're finished with the touchy-feely stuff," he said, frowning at Tiffany and Courtney, "please take your seats, and put your cellphones away. Unless you want to give me an early Christmas gift. I could use an upgrade." He smiled his grinchy grin.

Saved by the teacher.

Courtney sashayed to her desk, and Tiffany took the seat behind me. We hadn't spoken since the day I'd found her passed out in the bathroom. Was she still making herself throw up?

I hope not.

Purses zipped open and girls tucked their phones

inside. Boys pocketed their phones.

Mr. Hazzard didn't give second warnings, and we all knew it. He settled onto the corner of his desk, eyes squinting eagle-sharp, searching for someone who hadn't complied. "Also, this would be the time to disconnect any music you're listening to. We are here to study history. Take out your books, please. Now."

Thirty kids produced history books from their backpacks and sat at attention, waiting for the next direction. You didn't mess with a teacher who also handled detention.

A second later, I felt a tap on my shoulder and I turned, expecting Tiffany to call me Lard Butt or whisper some other endearing comment about how I'd maimed her best friend and didn't even apologize.

"You got an extra pencil?" Tiffany asked, without a trace of malice in her voice.

"I think so." I dug through my book bag and handed her one with a good eraser.

"Thanks."

And that was it. No speech. No harassment. No name calling.

"Miss Werthman?" Mr. Hazzard twirled a pen between his fingers like a miniature baton. "Is there something you'd like to share with the rest of us?"

I felt my face grow warm. Figured. Tiffany talked to me first, but I was the one who got in trouble. "No."

Mr. Hazzard's eyebrows shot up. "No? Well then, is it all right with you if we go on with the class? Because I certainly wouldn't want to interrupt an important conversation."

A bunch of kids laughed.

"We're done talking," I said.

More giggling. I couldn't blame Tiffany for this,

because the girl already hated me, so I did the only other thing I could think of...I smiled too, which was probably a gigantic mistake. Mr. Hazzard might misinterpret it as disrespect aimed at him.

"Good," Mr. Hazzard said. "Glad to hear it. Now, you'd all better take notes, because there will be a quiz over this material in one week." For the next hour, Mr. Hazzard lectured.

I could hardly write fast enough. When the bell rang, I flexed my fingers to get rid of the cramp in my hand.

"See you at soccer practice," Tiffany said, hurrying past me to catch up with Courtney.

Wow. She talked civilly to me. Treated me almost like an equal. I couldn't wait to tell Jonah and Jazz at lunchtime.

The morning went by fast, and I headed for the cafeteria. For once, the offerings in the lunch line resembled actual food: tacos, salad, green beans and cottage cheese with peaches. I pushed my tray along the counter and added a carton of one percent chocolate milk from the cooler at the end of the line. I paid, and then turned to see if Jonah or Jazz had arrived yet, but instead, I noticed Eli, loitering outside the entrance.

Go talk to him. I can't, people will think I'm weird. Well, tough. You told him you'd be his friend. Pasting a smile on my face, I carried my tray over to the doorway. "Hi. How's it going?" I had an urge to grab one of his arms, push his shirtsleeve up and check for fresh marks, but I knew I couldn't. Was he still cutting himself? Did he like Miss Gladden as much as I did?

A gap-toothed smile spread across Eli's pimply face. Threads hung from the hem of his long-sleeved shirt, and skin peeked through two holes in the fabric. "H-H-Hi Lauren. Fine."

"You want to sit at my table?"

"OK," he said, one part surprise, one part joy on his face.

It didn't take a whole lot of effort to make somebody's day. Yes, kids stared at us as Eli walked beside me before he drifted into the lunch line. Yes, kids whispered to each other. Some even pointed at me, but the strange thing was, I didn't care. Even if I'd committed social suicide, I'd done the right thing. I'd been brave. Stupid, maybe, but brave.

Eli scurried across the cafeteria and about tripped over his own feet, his lunch almost going airborne. Was he afraid I'd change my mind and tell him to get lost? Setting his tray down, he scooted next to me on the bench. He tore the wrapper off his straw, plunged it into his milk carton and slurped.

I'd be willing to bet, a lot, that nobody had ever invited him to sit with them. Sad. For all I knew, this was the best day of Eli Fleming's life. "So, how'd it go with Miss Gladden?" I asked.

"S-S-She's nice. I like her."

"Me too. Do you think it'll help?"

He nodded. "I...haven't done it since you found me in the art room."

"That's great, Eli!"

Blushing, he snatched a hard-shelled taco and bit into it, some filling oozing out onto his plate.

I glanced at the entrance, wishing Jonah or Jazz would show up, because sitting here alone with Eli, I knew I was really fueling the gossip machine.

Eli stopped chewing. "D-D-Do you want me to leave?"

"No."

"You…keep looking at the door."

"I was just wondering where Jonah and Jazz are. They're late."

He mopped up the mess at the corners of his mouth. "I-I-I can leave when they get here, if you want."

"Why? They won't care if you sit with us."

Eli smiled. Bits of food stuck to his teeth. "O-O-OK."

When I caught some kids at the next table staring at us, I gave them the biggest grin I could manage and took a bite of my own taco. Hey, according to Jonah, Jesus hung out with unpopular people too.

Fifteen minutes later, Jonah arrived and sat down next to me, which was awkward. My boyfriend was on one side and Eli Fleming was on the other. But I'd been right. Jonah didn't mind if Eli sat with us. In fact, he chatted with him the whole time and invited us both to his youth group meeting at church. This was like the tenth time he'd asked me, so I figured if it was so important to him, I should give it a try. Just this once.

"I'll go," I said.

"M-M-Me too," Eli said.

"Go where?" Jazz plopped her tray across from me and sat.

"To my youth group meeting tonight," Jonah said, grinning. "They're both coming. What about you?"

"I am Hindu, Jonah."

He shrugged. "So? You'd still be welcome."

She slugged him in the shoulder.

31

It had been a week since Mom checked herself into New Hope Rehab Center. On Saturday, Dad and I hopped into his truck to make the thirty-minute drive to go visit her. He powered on the radio, and drummed his fingers against the steering wheel, acting as normal as I'd seen him act for months. I winced as he strained to hit the high notes in the old song playing over the airways.

"Pretty good, huh?" He smiled. Crinkled skin framed his pale green eyes.

I laughed. "Sure, Dad. How long will Mom have to stay there?"

"Depends on her progress, but they said probably four to six weeks."

"I hope it's only four. No offense, but you can't cook." We'd had TV dinners every night since Mom left. I never thought I'd actually miss her salads and skinless baked chicken, but I did.

Dad's mouth drooped for a second but then twitched into a tiny smile. "You're welcome to make dinner any night you want."

"I have birthday money. How 'bout we go out to eat tonight?"

"How can I turn down a date with the second most beautiful girl in the world? I accept."

Second? Oh. Mom was first. He loved her. They'd work things out. They would.

We drove for miles without passing another vehicle. At a four-way intersection, we turned right. The truck tires crunched along a gravel road that snaked between fields of yellowed cornstalks, tall and brittle against the clear fall sky. An occasional farmhouse sprang into view.

Grain silos and windmills cast shadows on the thick-bladed grass bent by the wind. Around the next curve, cattle and horses grazed inside barbed-wire fencing.

"This place is out in the boonies," Dad said.

Finally, New Hope appeared on top of the next hill. It stood like an island, surrounded not by water but by grassy fields, looking more like a rest home than a rehab center. Rocking chairs lined the front porch. Potted ferns swayed in planters evenly spaced under the eaves, and a wind chime sang out, tickled by the breeze.

"This is it." Dad pulled the truck between the white lines in the parking area. "Ready?"

We jumped out and he threw his arm over my shoulder, his fingers squeezing reassuringly against me. Together we hiked to the front door of the sprawling, ranch-style building. I didn't know whether Mom had told him she'd left the pool gate open, but finding out I was only half responsible for Haley's death had allowed a small seed of hope to take root inside me. And today, walking with my dad, I dared to believe we could become a family again.

He reached up to ring the bell and the grapevine wreath hanging on the door swung back and forth, nearly falling off its hook.

"Yes?" a woman's voice came through the intercom box.

"We're here to see Mrs. Werthman," Dad said.

"Please come in." A buzzer sounded. Dad yanked on the door handle and it opened.

We stepped inside a pale blue room with beige-colored, over-stuffed furniture. One section of the huge space housed a dining area. Skinny vases holding single white carnations topped each table. On the other side of the room, several sitting areas had been arranged with couches and chairs facing each other, and coffee tables centered between them. Straight ahead, through an archway, was a pool table, and behind it were vending machines with pop and snacks, Mom's definition of junk food.

"Hello!" the brunette sitting behind the desk said. "Welcome. You need to sign in." She pointed to an open book with columns to list name, address, phone number and which resident you came to see. Pushing her chair back, she stood and circled around the desk. "I believe Mrs. Werthman is in the courtyard. If you'll have a seat over there, I'll tell her she has company."

I sat with my hands folded in my lap, wondering how Mom would look. For the first couple of days, I liked having her gone. The house was quiet, and Dad wasn't a member in good standing of the food police. But the weird thing was, I hadn't binged on chips or chocolate or ice cream since she left, and by eating the TV dinners, I'd even lost a couple of pounds.

We hadn't talked to Mom, because that was one of the rules here—no outside contact for the first week. She wasn't allowed to have a cellphone either, and she didn't have a phone in her room, although in an emergency, you could contact a resident by calling the main number.

Dad fidgeted in his chair. He leaned slightly

forward and cupped his hands over both knees like a runner pausing to catch his breath before he took off sprinting again. Was he nervous about seeing Mom? Had she missed him? Had she missed me?

The first thing I noticed was her clothes—a tee-shirt, faded jeans and loafers, no socks. I'd never seen her dress so casually. When she spotted us, she bolted across the room, almost colliding with another resident. Dad opened his arms and she fell inside them, fitting perfectly like a key gliding into a lock, and they stood wrapped tightly together, as if they were the only two people in the room.

They've found their way back to each other.

"Hi, Mom," I whispered.

My parents relaxed their hold and stepped apart. "Lauren," Mom said. "I'm glad you came."

There was a warmth in her voice, a tone I'd been longing to hear ever since Haley died. "Me too."

She led us to one of the sitting areas. She and Dad sat holding hands, facing me.

Everything was going to be OK. She looked better. The dark circles under her eyes were fading. New enthusiasm lit her face.

"Do you want something to drink, honey?" she asked me. "There're pop machines in the back."

What? Warning sirens blared inside my head. My mother never offered me pop. She never bought pop. It was on her "empty calorie" hit list.

Dad dug in his pockets for change. He produced six quarters and plopped them into my hand. "There you go. Get a pop."

I stood and looked from him to my mother—both their faces unreadable—and I wondered what was up. It was obvious they wanted me to disappear for a minute, but why? Shuffling across the room, I glanced over my shoulder. They were huddled together, talking, like football players whose coach had called a time out to discuss a new play.

They'd held hands. They'd hugged. They were OK, weren't they?

Loitering by the snack machines for a few minutes, I sipped my pop—regular not diet. I eyed the vending machines and considered buying a pack of peanuts or some peanut butter pieces, wondering if doing so would shake a normal reaction out of Mom.

As it turned out, I didn't need to buy a forbidden food. When I returned, Mom offered me one. "You guys have to stay for lunch," she said. "They make the best homemade pizza here. They smother it with extra cheese, and it has tons of toppings and the crust is light and flakey."

Fisting my hips, I stared down at them. "What's going on?"

Mom stole a quick glance at Dad. "You didn't tell her?"

He shook his head. "I thought we could talk about it over lunch."

I lost my appetite. "No, Dad, you can't say something like that and then drop it. You have to tell me now." I squeezed my eyes shut and offered a silent prayer to a God I'd just recently decided to contact: *Don't let them mention the word divorce.*

Mom reached for my hand. "I really think it'd be best to wait until lunchtime."

I shrugged out of her grasp. "Better for whom?" Every word rose a decibel, causing the other residents to stare at us, a Humpty Dumpty family who couldn't find a way to put itself back together again.

"OK," Mom said. "You win. But let's talk in my room."

Colorless and plain, the room screamed dull. I wondered how anybody could live here for weeks at a time. There was one chair with a vinyl seat. The bed was standard hospital issue with steel rails and a white non-fluffy spread.

Mom lowered the rails so she and Dad could sit on the bed, and I sank into the stiff-backed chair. One window dressed with mini-blinds offered a spectacular view of the parking lot and a row of dumpsters, trash spewing out of their mouths. A framed picture of a seagull, white feathers tinged with gray, hung on the wall opposite the bed.

I swallowed and picked at my nails, and my parents watched me, waiting for the right time, I guess, to ruin the scraps of hope I had left in my life.

Please don't say you're splitting up. Please. When I couldn't stand it a minute longer, I asked them flat out, "Are you getting a divorce?"

"What?" Dad asked, surprise evident in his voice. "No. We wanted to surprise you. We're taking a vacation, sweetheart. A cruise. To the Bahamas. Right after Christmas. How does that sound?"

Like heaven. "Really?"

"Come here," Mom said, reaching out to me.

We sat huddled together in that bland room, our arms wrapped around each other. My family was whole again. I'd never forget my sister. I'd never forget how she died. But I was finally ready to give myself permission to go on living.

Thank you for purchasing this Watershed Books title.
For other inspirational stories, please visit our on-line
bookstore at www.pelicanbookgroup.com.

For questions or more information, contact us at
customer@pelicanbookgroup.com.

Watershed Books
Make a Splash!™
an imprint of Pelican Ventures Book Group
www.PelicanBookGroup.com

Connect with Us
www.facebook.com/Pelicanbookgroup
www.twitter.com/pelicanbookgrp

To receive news and specials, subscribe to our bulletin
http://pelink.us/bulletin

May God's glory shine through
this inspirational work of fiction.

AMDG

CPSIA information can be obtained
at www.ICGtesting.com
Printed in the USA
FSOW01n1153061215
14065FS